IS THIS ANY WAY
TO RUN AN ARMY...?

We landed in a field north of the Lodonite army and waited over an hour for someone to come and meet us. Then we decided we'd waited long enough.

On the way to the camp we passed about half a dozen abandoned carts, scattered weapons, broken crockery. But there were no people anywhere until we rounded a curve in the road—and walked right into the army camp. At last we'd found people—but everyone was drunk! Of course, drunken soldiers were nothing new. But an *entire army?*

Ben: "Ten to one the Kamarians win the war."

No one took the bet. It seemed obvious that Kamaria was where we belonged, that we had chosen to visit the losers first. It wasn't until we got to Kamaria that we found out just how wrong a sure bet can be. . . .

More Science Fiction from SIGNET

BIBBLINGS

by
Barbara Paul

A SIGNET BOOK
NEW AMERICAN LIBRARY
TIMES MIRROR

SIGNET TRADEMARK REG. U.S. PAT. OFF. AND FOREIGN COUNTRIES
REGISTERED TRADEMARK—MARCA REGISTRADA
HECHO EN CHICAGO, U.S.A.

SIGNET, SIGNET CLASSICS, MENTOR, PLUME AND MERIDIAN BOOKS
are published by The New American Library, Inc.,
1301 Avenue of the Americas, New York, New York 10019

FIRST PRINTING, NOVEMBER, 1979

1 2 3 4 5 6 7 8 9

For my parents,
Evelyn and Kenneth Traber

1

Playtime was over.

I put both arms around Adam's waist and hugged so hard he grunted. "I'm not ready for this," I said.

He rested his chin on my head. "We don't know what 'this' is yet."

"Doesn't matter. Whatever, I'm not ready for it."

We'd been given three months this time, a sort of special bonus for A Job Well Done, thenkyew. Wasn't enough.

Adam de-opaqued the outside wall of the room and we stood looking down on Haldane Square—a graceful, formal park that made up the hub of the Corps Complex. Versailles remembered. A few people walking through the square, purposefully but not hurriedly. Nobody hurried here. Hurrying might suggest something had slipped out of control.

Nobody wasted time either; our three months' playtime was a programmed indulgence, a pressure valve to keep us sane and functioning. And now it was time to start doing a little of that functioning, to prove all over again how indispensable to the Corps we were. It got a little trickier each time.

Adam and I had checked into the suite provided by the Corps late last night. We'd slept and made love and eaten and made love and brushed our teeth and washed our hair and scrubbed each other's backs and made love and did everything else we could think of to prolong our illusion of leisure. They should have given us four months.

But we were in the busybody business and it was time to get busy. We were meeting the others first for a drink and how-was-your-vacation before reporting for our new assignment. Adam and I made our way down to the terrace cafe overlooking Haldane Square and chose a table for six.

It was pleasant there under the sky dome, a light artificial breeze playing over the terrace. The Diplomatic Corps Complex wasn't exactly a homey place, and visitors occasionally felt intimidated by the formality of its layout. Personally, I found it refreshing; it's nice to be reminded once in a while that chaos can be overcome.

Adam and I waited quietly, not talking; we'd already said out loud what we were both thinking. Several times. This mission was going to be different: a brand-new element was being introduced. No point in manufacturing anxieties before meeting up with the new element face to face. See what the others thought.

Alison and Ben Whitfield were the first to arrive, making their entrance in typical Whitfield fashion. What a pair. Ben: a big, shambling papa bear with a tendency to walk into tables and trip over flowers. Alison the Petite, all over the place, flitting here and there like a butterfly. A *disorganized* butterfly. Big Ben and tiny Alison: the kind of couple that dances cheek-to-belt. Together they made up the most brilliant medical team in the Diplomatic Corps' service.

The Whitfields lived double lives. In the laboratory they were orderly, fast-moving, inspired. Outside the laboratory was another story. I've known Ben to read a medical article once and then quote from it verbatim two years later. But ask him where he left his toothbrush and he stares at you so blankly, you start thinking he's waiting for you to explain what a toothbrush is.

They came in the end of the terrace opposite where Adam and I were sitting. Alison caught sight of us and flung up a hand in greeting—and scattered papers for five meters around. She made an oh-my-goodness face and bent over to pick up her papers. Ben, whose attention was elsewhere (Ben's attention was often elsewhere), didn't see Alison bending over and almost took a nosedive over her small body. But between them the Whitfields recovered all the papers (now slightly wrinkled) and carefully made their way past the remaining hazards on the terrace to our table.

"Valerie! Adam!" cried Alison.

"Adam! Valerie!" cried Ben.

And then they both fell on us as if we were long-lost family they hadn't seen for twenty years. It must have looked very naive and home-folks-get-together-meetin'-time, but that was part of the Whitfield style. It was one reason I liked them: they were open and enthusiastic and didn't have one jot of phoniness in them. They were honestly glad to see us, and we were glad to see them.

Chit-chatting, saying things friends and co-workers always say following a brief separation. Then Alison asked about Sondra and Will, the other couple on our team, and that question marked the official end of our vacation.

"There's been a change," I told the Whitfields. "Will won't be with us any more. He and Sondra were divorced the week after we left Gyges."

Alison and Ben stared at us open-mouthed, dismayed, unbelieving. *I know, I know:* the six of us had been together eleven years.

"But . . . but why?" Alison asked unhappily. "They certainly weren't having trouble when we were on Gyges. Were they?"

"Not that I could see," I said. "The trouble was Will. You know how he's been bellyaching about the Corps the past couple of years. Well, it was more than just bellyaching. He was truly unhappy with his work. After we left Gyges, Will told Sondra he wanted to quit the Corps. She refused to quit with him, and so they agreed to divorce. Just like that."

Ben whistled. "That's scary. Like having a relative up and resign from the family."

Exactly.

"So there are only five people on our team now?" Alison said dubiously.

"Six as usual," Adam said. "Sondra has a new husband. He'll be coming with us."

They puzzled over that for a moment. Then Ben asked, "You mean he's been assigned to our team just because he's Sondra's husband? The Culloden permitted it?"

"Not quite like that," said Adam. "It seems he has some special knowledge that'll be helpful to us—the Culloden sounded quite pleased to announce his appointment."

I touched Adam's arm. "The marriage probably helped. You know the Culloden likes to use married couples more than mix-and-match singles. Tidier."

Ben laughed. "Count on Sondra to make a practical choice. What's his name?"

"Justin Bark."

"Bark? As in dog?"

Adam grinned. "As in dog."

Ben shook his head. "What did they choose for their married name?"

"*That's* their married name. Justin's original name was Elliott. I don't know why they chose Bark."

"Sondra Bark." Alison, trying it out, trying to like it.

Ben: "What's this special knowledge Justin Bark's supposed to have?"

"He's an expert on mountain warfare," said Adam. "That means there'll be fighting wherever they're sending us."

Totally unconscious of what they were doing: Alison and Ben drawing together a little when they heard we were being sent to a planet where fighting was going on. Protecting each other, sharing the responsibility. Men like Ben Whitfield tended to marry smug, super-efficient women who'd smile indulgently on their little-boy husbands all the time they were taking care of them. And the Alison Whitfields of the human race often found themselves under the thumbs of cock-of-the-walk types who used their wives to boost their own faltering egos. Parent-child marriages, unwholesome and repressive. But

Alison and Ben had managed to find each other and avoid that trap. Because they were so good at what they *wanted* to be good at, they had no need of a mommy or a daddy.

"D'you suppose that's why Sondra married him?" Ben, still thinking about Justin Bark's special qualifications for this mission. "Just to have a . . . a working partner on this tour?"

"Not on your life," said Alison, wide-eyed. "Take a look."

We took a look: I saw what Alison meant. Sondra and her new husband were just coming onto the terrace and Justin Bark was, to put it bluntly, the most beautiful man I'd ever laid eyes on. Dark hair and eyes, good skin, imposing stature, athlete's build and dancer's moves—all the storybook graces. Masculine. Ohwowgeewhiz*yes* masculine. Men who walk around exuding virility usually give me the giggles, but not this one. Sondra was a good-looking woman, but it was her husband the other people on the terrace were turning to stare at. Justin Bark was definitely not a man you marry because you want to *work* with him.

I nudged Adam. "Give up."

Adam sighed and rose to welcome the newcomers. Sondra looked good—healthy and happy and getting a kick out of our reaction to Justin. Slightly self-conscious conversation, unsubtle attempts at getting acquainted with this stranger with whom we'd be living on fairly intimate terms for the next few months. Because we were the senior pair of the team, Adam and I had been notified earlier of Justin's appointment. For the sake of form, our consent was required. We'd studied the man's background and experience, but of course that didn't really explain the man himself. Ultimately we'd signed the consent form simply because Sondra had chosen him.

Right now Justin was handling his difficult position about as well as could be expected. He knew he was being looked over and evaluated by his wife's best friends. None of us had had to come into a closed group like that—Justin was bound to feel odd man out for a while.

You could tell he wanted to like us and he wanted us to like him. But he couldn't beg for approval. Nor could we.

"I was a historian before I joined the Corps," he was saying. "Military history. But there's only so much you can learn from tapes. I needed to see some real fighting for myself."

"So he became a diplomat," Sondra laughed.

But if Justin was in a ticklish spot, so were the rest of us. Before Sondra and Will had divorced, we'd been six extremely lucky people. Because each of us had found other people we could trust. Take me: I knew five people whom I trusted implicitly, had, in fact, trusted with my life on more than one occasion. *Five* of them. How many people go through life without finding even *one* person they can trust without reservation? In our line of work, if you can't depend on the other guy you might as well pack up and go home. And that's why we were willing to accept Justin now: we trusted Sondra's judgment. You knighted we stand.

Nevertheless Justin was an unknown. A new note being sounded.

"Do you know where we're going?" Sondra asked me.

"Haven't a clue. The Culloden's being even more tight-lipped than usual."

"Speaking of," said Adam, looking at his wrist.

"Already?" Alison, surprised. "But we've been here only ten minutes!"

"We've been here an hour," I laughed. "Come on. Let's go see what the Corpse wants us to do this time."

"Some day you're going to forget and say that in front of some Corps official who'll never forgive you," Adam said.

"Never," I assured him. "I'm not suicidal."

2

"Well, well, well, well, and well. If it isn't the Anglo-Saxon Invaders. Right on time, too."

"Hello, Pilcer, how are you?" Adam said pleasantly, hiding his annoyance at the epithet.

Justin looked confused.

"Oh, I keep on keeping on," said Pilcer. "This must be your new member—Justin Bark, isn't it? My name's Pilcer. I'm Director Culloden's executive assistant. Ready to take up your share of the white man's burden?"

Justin looked more confused than ever.

"Didn't you tell him?" I said to Sondra, low.

Head-shake. "I hoped all that would have died down by now."

Adam stepped in smoothly. "Say, Pilcer, I've been meaning to ask you . . ." He drew the assistant off into a private conversation.

I knew a cue when I saw one. I motioned to Justin and he followed me to a corner seat away from Adam and Pilcer.

"What was that about Anglo-Saxon invaders?" he asked as we sat down.

"A little nickname we've picked up," I said. "You're new to the service so you haven't run into it yet. The Diplomatic Corps is very, very touchy about any suggestion of clannishness within its ranks. The Federation wants all its more visible agencies to show peoples from various worlds working together in harmony, hands-across-the-skies, that sort of thing. And the Diplomatic Corps is just a little more visible than most. Our team is different from the others—we're the only team in the Corps whose ancestors all came from the same planet. Not only that, we don't even represent a racial mix of our own species. Where did your ancestors come from, Justin?"

"England."

I spread my hands. "There you are. The only reason the Culloden hasn't reassigned all of us to different teams is that we have such a good track record. He knows we work well together."

"Why do you call him *the* Culloden?" Justin asked absently.

"Because he likes to be thought of as an institution. We try to oblige." Justin grinned at me. "Culloden won't do anything so crude as call us Anglo-Saxon Invaders to our face," I went on. "But if he starts hinting we're on a sort of perpetual probation, I want you to know why."

"Trying to warn me off?"

"Good lord, no," I laughed. "But we are resented here. It's reverse discrimination, of course, and there's not a damned thing we can do about it. A lot of the good folk in the Corps think we're a special-privilege group when in fact just the opposite's true. We have to prove ourselves all over again every time we're sent out—just to keep from being disbanded." I paused to make sure he understood the importance of what I was telling him. "We're not allowed to fail, Justin."

He expelled a breath he'd been holding. "I didn't know any of this."

"Would it have made a difference?" I asked, curious.

He grinned again. "No."

I didn't tell Justin, but I doubted that there would have been so much criticism of us if we'd all come from Nisa or Gyges or Sirius II. Earth culture had dominated the Federation just long enough for a little resentment to begin to surface. Our literature had had to struggle with the vagaries of translation as all literatures everywhere must, but Earth art and music had survived the test of time and space and were recognized in most parts of the known galaxy. People to whom art was just a frivolous decoration were beginning to express their scorn openly; others were more subtle. Our diplomatic team was resented within the Corps not just because we all shared the same heritage, but because that heritage was *Earth's* heritage.

"And just what are you two tête-à-tête-ing about?" said Pilcer's voice from above us. Across the room: Adam, palms up, *couldn't-hold-him-any-longer*.

I looked up at Culloden's assistant. "I was telling him all about your scandalous sex life," I said deadpan.

Pilcer looked coyly pleased. "Now, now, Valerie, we mustn't carry tales. I'm sure you have better things to talk about. Welcoming your new member, for instance. Checking his bloodlines." Smirk.

"Pilcer, is it true," Sondra asked innocently, "that you're Culloden's natural son?" *Take that!*

Pilcer's face turned pink; he'd run into that particular canard before. Implication: How else could such a horse's ass hold on to an important job for so long?

"I swear," Pilcer exploded, "I cannot understand why they call you people *diplomats!*"

We all burst out laughing. Ben Whitfield clapped Pilcer clumsily on the shoulder. "Just a little fun. No harm meant."

Adam, whose designated job was piloting our ship, just happened to be the only true diplomat in the bunch. (Unless Justin Bark should turn out to have smoother-over talents.) Adam had that rare gift of being able to step into an awkward situation and say exactly the right thing to ease everybody's tensions. His father had had the same gift. Me, I grew up in a blurt-it-out family.

Being called a diplomat doesn't automatically guarantee that one is diplomatic. In the past our team would have been called trouble-shooters or problem-solvers, old-fashioned labels the Corps considered needlessly self-congratulatory and a bit tacky. So we were called diplomats. It was good for a giggle.

A signal light flashed over Pilcer's desk. "The Director will see you now," Pilcer said, recovering his poise. Down a hallway to the holy-of-holies, chief roosting place of the

Director of the Diplomatic Corps of the Federation of United Worlds. (Tautology typical.) Pilcer ushered us into the inner sanctum, announcing: "The Chester Commission, Director. Valerie Chester. Adam Chester." He didn't name the others; in Pilcer's hierarchy of values only the senior pair were worthy of that honor. Pilcer saw us all in and withdrew.

A figure rising from behind a desk: tall, slim, elegant, totally white from head to foot. White clothing, chalk-white skin. No rosy cheeks, no blue veins showing through. Hairless. Eyes two slits which closed from the bottom upward. Culloden was, literally, unique: he was the first and so far only offspring of a mating between an Earthwoman and a male of the Takran race on Olliman's World.

He flowed toward us, murmuring greetings and making sure we all found comfortable seats. When he had us arranged to suit him, he said, "I haven't had a chance to congratulate you personally on the way you handled that dreadful business on Gyges. Border disputes can be so messy, can't they? But all the contending parties seem satisfied with the arrangement you worked out. The Corps is quite pleased with your work."

"Thank you, Director," I said. "The job was less difficult than we'd anticipated." The Corps encourages modesty in its representatives. (As a matter of fact, Gyges had turned out to be a piece of cake; but I didn't see any reason to tell the Director *that*.)

"Good, good," Culloden murmured. "I knew I could count on you. You haven't let us down yet—an enviable record, enviable. You've proved once again what effective bargaining units married couples make—I don't know why my predecessors never thought of it." He cleared his throat, trying not to sound too pleased with his own foresight. "I sometimes think just the *ritual* of marriage helps make a good impression on people we're negotiating with. Ceremony implies permanence, stability. We should take advantage of everything that helps the Corps present an appearance of stability, don't you think?"

Oh yes we did indeed yes. It wasn't a matter of morality. Culloden didn't give a hoot about our morals, ours or anybody else's. The inevitable couplings that went on during long tours couldn't have interested him less: just so it was all kept behind closed doors. All that interested the Director was results. Since the use of married couples on diplomatic missions was Culloden's pet project, we could feel relatively certain our careers were safe.

More or less.

"I'm especially pleased when *your* team succeeds," Culloden beamed at us. "I understand the pressure you're under must be annoying—but you don't really let that nasty Anglo-Saxon Invaders business bother you, do you? The Corps doesn't mind winking at the Federation directive concerning cultural mix when we have a team as successful as yours." His eye slits closed upward; that was Culloden's way of smiling. "And you'll continue to be successful, I'm sure."

Meaning: We'd better be.

An odd situation. Culloden's own claim to uniqueness—his mixture of Earth and Takran genes—predisposed him to frown on any group under his command that might reflect cultural bias. (Friendship toward some can so easily be mistaken for intolerance toward others.) But Culloden was too ambitious a man to let personal preference interfere with what so far had proved to be a winning game: when we looked good, he looked good.

To Justin, he said: "I'm so glad you've decided to join us. We've had our eye on you for some time now, you know." To all of us: "I'm sure you must be eager to learn about your new assignment, so I won't keep you waiting. It could be difficult, we don't really know. But of all our diplomatic teams, I think yours is the best equipped to handle this particular problem."

Which meant we probably were, immodest as that sounds. Culloden was a sort of diplomatic casting genius; he unerringly picked the right people for the right job time after time. That's one reason he was director of the Corps.

"We're sending you to Lodon-Kamaria," he said, and waited.

Surreptitious exchange of glances: *Have you heard of it?*

"Is it a Federation world, Director?" Adam asked.

"No, it isn't. In fact, the Federation didn't even know it existed until thirty-four subjective years ago. It's a small planet with only two nations, both living on the same landmass. The landmass is divided by a low mountain range running north and south, beginning and ending in polar regions. East of the mountains is the nation of Lodon. To the west, Kamaria."

"Two languages?" Sondra asked.

"No, just one. Lodonites and Kamarians are the same race, but half of them live on one side of the mountains and half on the other. And here's the unpleasant part: they're in a perpetual state of war."

Thus Justin Bark.

Culloden continued, "The first scouting parties the Federation sent out reported that hostilities seemed to ease up about twice a year, but they never ceased altogether. We don't know why they're fighting. No territorial advance seems to be involved."

"Technology?" Sondra again.

"None. Lodon-Kamaria is rated 5.1 on the Denner scale."

I smothered a laugh when I saw Sondra struggling to keep her face expressionless. Sondra *hated* underdeveloped worlds; there wasn't one drop of pioneering blood in her veins. She said all that politely expressed admiration for world settlers and civilization builders was just so much horse manure. Especially when that admiration was directed toward women who bore seventeen children and fought the wilderness every day and worked like coolies from dawn to dusk. Sondra claimed those women had no more choice in the matter than the other breed animals their husbands drove before them. Why make a virtue of such an ugly business?

Culloden noticed Sondra's reaction and gave his eye-slit smile; he didn't miss much. "The Lodonites and the Kamarians fight their war in the mountains—the natural boundary between the two nations. That's why we're so pleased to have an expert on mountain fighting on the team." He nodded pleasantly toward Justin. "After reviewing the scouting parties' reports thirty-four years ago, the Federation decided on a policy of nonintervention."

The corners of the Director's mouth turned down. There was a rivalry between the Diplomatic Corps and the Council responsible for determining top-level Federation policy; Culloden didn't always approve of Federation Council decisions. He said: "The Council grandly announced that whatever the quarrel between the Lodonites and the Kamarians, it was nobody's business but their own. That way the Federation managed, one, to avoid thinking about the problem. Two, not to pour money into somebody else's war. Three, to keep its own hands clean. All at the same time. No official representative of the Federation has visited the planet for nearly thirty years."

But private individuals had, Culloden told us, including geologists and industrial prospectors. They discovered that the planet's battleground, the mountain range, was rich with alphidium deposits. Alphidium meant nothing to the Lodonites and the Kamarians. They heated their homes by burning wood in their fireplaces; they had no interstellar ships to fuel.

"The alphidium will be impossible to mine in the midst of a war," said Culloden. "The only way to get at this precious ore is through the cooperation of both warring factions."

The Federation Council thus proclaimed that its earlier policy of nonintervention had shown a certain insensitivity to the sufferings of people inhabiting non-Federation worlds. The Diplomatic Corps was instructed to dispatch a peace commission to help the Lodonites and the Kamarians resolve their differences.

"The Council's wishes aren't always in touch with the reality of a situation," said Culloden. "Of course we don't expect you to stop the war. Your specific instructions are as follows. Find out why the Lodonites and the Kamarians are fighting. Recommend specific steps the Federation can take to end the hostilities. If you judge a truce to be infeasible, recommend which nation the Federation should side with in the struggle. Once Federation technology moves in, the war will be over in a matter of hours."

He looked at us carefully. "You understand that the last possibility is to be considered only as a last resort. The Council wants to avoid taking sides if at all possible, and in that they're absolutely right." Slit-eyed smile. "I'm sure you'll come up with some more palatable solution."

I wished I was that sure.

"I'm afraid your hypnobriefing won't be as thorough as we'd like," said the Director. "We have the language on tape, of course. And a little something of geography and social customs. Life is a bit grim on Lodon-Kamaria, I gather. The people have little they can call their own since the war has first claim on anything of value. No systematic study of the available foods has ever been made. We know a few of the edibles, but the Doctors Whitfield will want to test everything before you eat it, I'm sure."

Alison and Ben nodded in unison; they would have tested the food anyway.

"Well, then, I think that takes care of everything? Unless you have a question."

I had a dozen. But Culloden was ready to dismiss us, so I rose and said, "I think we understand, Director. An interesting assignment." Cool and noncommittal, that's me.

"You can find your way out, then?"

We could find our way out. We said goodbye to Pilcer as we went through the reception chamber; he picked up a stylus from his desk and pointed it at us like a spear.

"Charge," he said.

3

"I think we're damned lucky," Adam said on our way to hypnobriefing. "Culloden could have sunk us. He could have given us an impossible assignment we'd be sure to fail—but instead he hands us evaluation and recommendation. The easiest trip of all."

"Why is that?" Justin the newcomer.

"Because even if you pull a boner with your recommendation, it usually doesn't catch up with you for a few years. By then you've got a couple more missions under your belt—successful ones, if you're lucky. In this business, it's only what you did on your *last* mission that counts."

"Oh," said Justin, not sure how to take this.

"I think the Culloden's trying to help us," Adam went on. "At least until this criticism of our common background dies down."

"I hope you're right," I said. "But don't you think it sounds a little *too* cushy? Evaluate and recommend. We haven't had an assignment like that in years."

"Valerie the pessimist," Alison smiled.

Maybe. I just wasn't convinced that making recommendations was all the Culloden really expected of us. A peace treaty would be nice. Frosting on the cake. (Also delusions of grandeur?) Adam was undoubtedly right, though; I probably only imagined I'd caught the odor of fish.

The woman in charge of our hypnobriefing was a

Strygmanite from Canopus IV whom I'd known for nine
years and disliked for ten. When Sondra introduced her to
Justin, she stared at him rudely.

"You're an Earthman," she said.

"My ancestors came from Earth," Justin replied. "I
was born on New Susa."

"I heard Sondra had married a Gygean."

She'd heard nothing of the sort. It was just another Anglo-Saxon Invaders needle. I reminded the woman that we
had a new language to learn among other things and
asked her to hook us up. We'd keep coming back to the
machines until all six of us felt comfortable with our new
learning.

Not that there was all that much to learn. The Culloden had said our hypnobriefing wouldn't be especially
thorough, and he was right. We did learn that Lodon-Kamaria was a small, moonless planet with three large land-
masses, only one of which supported intelligent life in any
number. A few people had made scattered attempts to
settle on islands and the other two continents, but as yet
their effect on the population distribution was negligible.
For practical purposes, Lodonite-Kamarian life was
concentrated around the mountain range that split the
main continent.

The people were not primitive, but they were preindus-
trial. Manufacturing was still in the artisan stage Ac-
cording to the early scouting reports, life on both sides of
the mountains was motivated by the need to keep the two
struggling armies supplied. These people lived for their
war.

There was no marriage on Lodon-Kamaria. People
grouped together in family units, but there was no ceremony to sanctify the union. This was odd. Civilizations
ranking 5.1 on the Denner scale almost invariably had a
great deal of ceremony woven into their social fabric. Ceremonies covering the weather, the crops, giving birth and
dying—ceremonies for building homes, for digging wells,
even for cutting down trees. But Lodon-Kamaria had no
ceremony for marriage.

Possibly because the Lodonite-Kamarian race gave

birth to three genders instead of the more ordinary two? Early rough estimate: neuters made up one-third of the population—not mutants, not a fluke, but a permanent part of the demographics of the planet. Z chromosome? A reasonable guess.

The language was not an especially complicated one—only five verb tenses, for instance. The Lodonites and the Kamarians had more than one word for things that were important to them—there was no single word meaning "water," for example. There was a word for rainwater and another for well water and a third for river water and so on. But they had only one word to name all the arts—music, painting, poetry, whatever else they might have, all lumped together in one category with one label. Draw your own conclusions.

The few subtleties of the language were mostly concentrated on the correct form of direct address, of all things. We learned that on Lodon-Kamaria all men (including offworld visitors such as the three men on our team) were to be addressed as *mirhilancthon,* which translated as "sire" as well as we could understand it. "Sire" in the literal sense of the word—one-who-fathers-children.

Mirhiliptha was the term used in addressing a woman —one-who-bears-children. They were both more than just descriptive terms—they implied respect. The nearest Earth equivalent we could come up with for *mirhiliptha* was the old German *gnädige Frau*—gracious Lady, esteemed Madam.

Sondra Bark objected. "It's patronizing," she said. "I don't want to be 'respected' because I'm a potential baby factory. Why do they make such a religion out of doing what any animal can do?"

"We'll find that out when we get there," I said. "In the meantime, *mirhiliptha* is meant as a term of honor and that's the way we'll take it. Smile and try to look honored."

"I don't know if I can."

"Smile."

Sondra stretched back her lips. "It hurts."

There was also a third form of address, *mirhilaves,* for

speaking to neuters. We guessed that had to mean one-who-does-not-father-or-bear-children. Was there a stigma attached to being nonreproductive? We didn't know.

As soon as he felt he could, Adam left the hypno-machines and went to the docking station to check out our ship. We'd been assigned a JX-31 equipped with a small laboratory for the Whitfields. The JX-31 was not an interstellar ship; those monster vessels required expensive outlays and large crews to make them go. Adam could pilot the JX-31 within a stellar system by himself. A space ferry would take us to Vayner (the Lodonite-Kamarian name for their star) and turn us loose. Adam would put the JX-31 into orbit around Lodon-Kamaria and we'd go down to the planet's surface in a shuttle.

Adam grumbled for several days while he struggled with Federation red tape trying to get some piece of equipment changed. But eventually he just threw up his hands in exasperation and okayed the JX-31 as it was. Nobody but Justin paid much attention; Adam always grumbled about his ships.

The cabins on the JX-31 were small but adequate. We laced ourselves in for liftoff and soon we were scooped up into the belly of the huge ferry. In the slot next to ours was a Federation scout ship, undoubtedly headed for some supersecret destination on some mysterious and important mission. We would stay inside the JX-31 all the way to Vayner, complaining loudly because the ferry provided no passenger facilities. All the ferry did was shift interplanetary ships from star to star. It didn't even sell hot dogs.

"What was it you were trying to get changed?" Justin asked Adam.

"The shuttle. Come on down and take a look."

We all followed Adam through the crawl chute to the shuttle. Inside the shuttle, the Whitfields and Sondra and I moaned and laughed. It was a twelve-passenger, single-control model instead of the six-passenger model we usually had.

"What's wrong with it?" Justin wanted to know.

"I requested two smaller shuttles," Adam explained,

"so we could split up if we wanted to. Instead they give us just one that's twice as large as we need." He slipped into the pilot's seat. "Gather round, chillun. The controls are the same as for the six-passenger shuttle with one exception. There's an extra deceleration stage. Here. But it has an automatic lock on it—there's no danger you'll skip the inserted stage and go on to the next. You can all handle it without any trouble." He looked at our newcomer. "Justin, I forget—can you drive one of these things?"

Justin nodded; he could fly a shuttle.

"You know, Adam, this might not be so bad," said Ben, stretching out his seventh of a ton over two seats. "We always felt cramped in a six-seater."

"*You* always felt cramped in a six-seater," Sondra laughed.

Justin was looking around the shuttle, grinning. "Here we are, sitting inside this ship which is inside another ship which is inside *another* ship."

Chinese boxes had nothing on us.

By the time the ferry reached Vayner we were all beginning to get the fidgets. The ferry pointed us in the general direction of Lodon-Kamaria and the JX-31 floated free. It took us four days to reach orbit, and we planned to circle the planet another full day to announce our arrival. Neither the Lodonites nor the Kamarians had developed radio, so there was no way to contact them and say, "We're here!" They had known for nearly thirty-five years that there was life on other planets, but they'd still find it a bit disconcerting to look out the window and see a space shuttle parked in the front yard. Orbiting another day (about twenty hours here) was to let the Lodonites and the Kamarians get used to the idea that they were going to have company.

Adam piloted us in low enough that the JX-31 scanners could pick up a good picture. Lodon-Kamaria was a pretty place, a hazy bluish-green for the most part. One of the unsettled continents had a wide stretch of pink desert in it, but most of the planet was heavily forested, even the islands. It was the largest landmass that we were

interested in, the one where the fighting was going on.
The mountain range that separated Lodon from Kamaria
was a long puckered blue scar beneath us. It was also a
source of great wealth if only the Lodonites and the Kamarians knew it.

When the time came, Adam took the controls of the
shuttle and the JX-31 spit us out like a melon seed. Back
and forth across the mountains half a dozen times: a
knock on the door. Would one nation be offended that we
visited the other one first? Relieved, more likely.

Justin Bark, evidently thinking along the same lines:
"Where are we going? We haven't even decided which nation we're visiting first!"

"Our first decision," I said.

"How do we decide?"

"Show him, Adam."

Adam fished out a small bronze disc and held it up for
all to see. It was an artifact, a coin left behind by a civilization on Pollux II that had vanished long before the
Federation had been formed. That coin had traveled with
us to many worlds.

Adam: "Call it, Val."

"Heads, Lodon—tails, Kamaria," I said.

Adams flipped the coin.

Heads it was. We were going to Lodon.

4

Take some of the blue out of the green and we could
have been in a Constable landscape—busy skies, trees
like monuments, a shimmering lushness everywhere you
looked.

We were in Lodon, but where were the Lodonites?
Adam had put us down in an open field north of the Lodonite army camp, and we'd been waiting over an hour
for someone to come meet us. (Bad manners to go nosing
around somebody else's planet without saying please and
thank you first.) No one had witnessed our landfall except a couple of bucolic types lolling on a nearby hillside.
They'd made no move toward us.

"I don't understand it," said Adam. "We were visible
from the army camp—they must know we're here. And
look at those two lounging over there—they couldn't care
less."

"You'd think they were visited by offworlders every
day," I said. "Most peculiar."

"Maybe they just haven't had time to get here yet,"
Sondra suggested.

Adam shrugged. "Can't be more than a twenty-minute
walk. Let's give our pastoral pals a try." He lifted an arm
and called out the Lodonite equivalent of "Hello, there."
No response.

"This isn't working the way it's supposed to," I said.
"I think we'd better take the initiative, don't you?"

Adam agreed. "Alison! Ben! We're going." The Whitfields had spent the hour examining the soil and various plants in the vicinity of the shuttle. Ben: a portable food analyzer strapped to his back, in case anyone should offer us tea and crumpets.

We wanted to find a man named Zizzi, the commander of the Lodonite army. Since Lodon had a military government, with all civic needs subordinated to those of the war, Zizzi was by extension the head of the government as well. We'd visited other places where the generals ran the country, and the results were invariably less than ideal. But ours was not to reason why, ours was but to evaluate and recommend.

The army camp lay due south of where we were, but there didn't seem to be a road. "Do you think those two could tell us the easiest way to get there?" I asked Adam.

"We can find out."

Tramp, tramp, tramp across the field to meet our first Lodonites. One of them turned out to be asleep; the other watched us idly, without much interest. His face was so sun-and-wind-burned it was hard to guess his age; this one had spent most of his life out of doors. Eyes: unfocused, seeing but not seeing. Clothing: filthy. He stank.

"Hello," I said to him. "We're—"

But before I could say any more the man stretched out his arm, pointed a skinny finger, and began jabbering at me, spittle running down his chin. I couldn't understand a word he said.

"Excuse me? If you'll slow down a little—"

"Forget it, Val," said Ben Whitfield. "He's drunk as a lord." As if to prove Ben right, the Lodonite dropped his arm and passed out, keeling over gracefully beside his sleeping friend. We left them both there, snoring away.

"Deserters?" I asked Adam.

But it was Justin who answered. "No. Too close to the camp. Even for runaway drunks."

Ben Whitfield walked into a patch of thistles, backed off, and led the rest of us on a wide detour that brought us to a dirt road heading south. It was a dirty dirt road, and before long we were one huge cloud of dust advancing on the Lodonite army camp. What a great first impression *we* were going to make.

On the way we passed about half a dozen abandoned carts. One of them had a broken axle, but the others all looked in good condition. A few weapons lay scattered in our path—a broken longbow here, an axhead there. Broken crockery, some pieces still recognizable as parts of jugs. And once: a pile of clothing, about two meters high, smack dab in the middle of the road. No people anywhere.

"What a haphazard way to run a war," Adam remarked.

Justin: "Looks more like the aftermath of war—all this debris, no people in sight. Probably hiding."

"You mean the war's over?" asked Alison.

"Could be."

We rounded a curve in the road—and walked right into the army camp. A wide expanse of buildings, all permanent structures: low, squat, gripping the ground as if afraid of being torn away. Pack animals, weapons, barrels of supplies, things we didn't recognize. And, at last, people.

Every blessed one of them was drunk.

The roadside ditches were filled with men and women sleeping it off. One woman lay stretched out in the road, crooning softly to herself. Near her, two men struggled feebly for the possession of a jug. In the middle distance: men and women reeling, shouting, sometimes stepping on sleeping figures on the ground. Some were ugly-drunk, some were peaceful. But drunk they were.

"Must have been quite a party," Adam said dryly.

"But was it a victory celebration or one final toot before surrendering?" said Justin. He looked worried. "Look, I know I'm the new boy on the team, but I don't think we ought to go waltzing in there as if nothing were wrong. It's obvious something has happened. There could be danger. I think we'd better leave the road and scout out the place before we try to make contact with Commander Zizzi."

Alison: "You mean sneak in?"

"I mean sneak in."

"Good idea," I said. "Lead the way."

Playing at commandos: follow Justin, hide behind a building, rush to that clump of trees, crouch beside a cart loaded with moldering fodder, tippy-toe up to a pile of logs. At last Justin stood up and walked out into the open, satisfied. "The Kamarian army might come swooping down out of the mountains at any moment," he said, "but there's no danger from these people."

We stood in the middle of the camp and looked around us. Drunken soldiers were nothing new. But an *entire army*? We picked our way among sprawling figures, some whimpering, some asleep in their own vomit. A pack animal lowed piteously over its empty feed box—a six-legged, broad-backed creature that Adam untied and led to a fodder cart. The debris we'd encountered on the road was multiplied a thousandfold here: smashed barrels, broken weapons, shattered jugs. The remains of what might have been an enormous block and tackle and a couple of pulleys. Carts without wheels. Wheels without carts. Shreds of clothing and blankets. A cracked whetstone. And more.

Justin kicked at a pile of rusty iron strips. (For barrel hoops?) "This didn't happen overnight. Look at that rust. Neglect, sheer neglect."

"Maybe the Lodonites like long orgies," I said.

He shook his head. "No, it's more than that. There hasn't been any discipline here for a long time. How can you run an army without discipline?"

Ben: "Ten to one the Kamarians win the war."

No one took the bet. This Lodonite army could have been conquered by a determined group of preschoolers.

A happy drunk lurched out of one of the buildings and tried to wrap his arms around Alison. Ben picked him up gently, carried him back into the building, shut the door. "Stinks in there." Wasn't exactly a rose garden outside, either.

"Look!" Sondra exclaimed, pointing.

At some distance two thin boys were moving among the drunken soldiers. One pushed a sort of pot mounted on wheels. The other ladled something out of the pot which he'd try to get a soldier to swallow.

"A drunk-feeding patrol?" Justin, incredulous.

We started running toward them. The two boys saw us, exchanged a nervous look.

"Wait!" I called. "Please don't go away! We just want to talk!"

The boys were torn between caution and curiosity. They stared at us as we hurried up to them, taking it all in—our clothing, our indoorsy alien look, Lord knows what else.

"Thank you for waiting," I panted. "We are strangers in Lodon, offworlders come to visit. Could you tell us what's happened here?"

One boy's eyes grew large while the other boy broke into a huge grin. The big-eyed boy said, "You came in a spaceship, mirhiliptha?"

"Yes. You didn't see our ship?"

The grinning boy elbowed his friend like boys everywhere. "See, I told you."

"But what's happened here?" I repeated.

The two boys looked around with a puzzled air. "Where, mirhiliptha?"

"Here in the camp," Adam said. "The entire army seems to be . . ." He paused. The language tapes had included no word for "intoxicated." An unmentionable? "They seem to have been drinking."

The boys looked at him uncomprehendingly. "But all the men and women in Lodon are drinking, mirhilancthon," one of them said.

"You're not," I pointed out. The whole country was drunk?

"We're neuters," was the answer.

So. Not boys after all. "Don't neuters drink?"

"We have no need to, mirhiliptha." As if that explained everything.

Save it for later. "We're looking for Commander Zizzi. Do you know where he is?"

They pointed to a building flying a plain black banner. That's all it was: black cloth, no insignia. We thanked the two young neuters and walked away toward the Commander's headquarters.

"I can see where we're going to have to be careful," I said to the others. "I didn't have a clue those two weren't boys."

"Boys?" Three heads swiveled to look at me. "I thought they were girls," said Adam. Ben and Justin had too.

I looked to the women. "I thought they were boys," Sondra nodded. Alison agreed.

Hm. Male vs. female views of neuterdom? Something else that would have to be saved for later.

The door to Commander Zizzi's headquarters building had been ripped out of its frame and was lying in a mud puddle, leaving one wooden hinge dangling from the frame. An obstacle in the doorway: a middle-aged woman, lying on her back, her head at a peculiar angle.

Alison bent over her. "Just drunk." She moved the woman's head to a more comfortable position.

Not much point in knocking on a door that's lying ten meters away from the building it's supposed to be attached to, so I stuck my head through the door frame and called, "Commander Zizzi?" No answer. I called again and stepped gingerly over the middle-aged woman into the building, made room for the others.

We were in a small windowless room decorated in Early Destruction. A broken table, three or four broken chairs, a couple of shattered oil lamps. A piece of map on the wall. Three other rooms opened out of the room we were in. Two were empty; in the third Commander Zizzi rose from a chair to receive us.

The man was stark naked.

He must have been nearly seventy and was skinny as a blowpipe. His hands and shoulders twitched and his eyes burned holes into us. I apologized for intruding and started to back out when he threw out an arm to stop me. "Spaceship? Spaceship?"

Yes, I told him.

He picked up a spear with a broken shaft and pointed

it at me and then gestured imperiously toward a low stool beneath the room's one window.

"I think he's inviting you to sit down," Adam said dryly.

I sat down. I've encountered a few unusual customs on the various worlds we've visited, but never had I seen one that required its military commander to receive diplomatic envoys in the buff. (I would have taken his word that he wasn't carrying a concealed weapon.) If Commander Zizzi had been a young man instead of an elderly one, the situation would at least have been interesting. As it was, it was merely ludicrous. We all managed to keep a straight face, and settled down to talk.

We did all the talking. We didn't plan it that way, but all we could get out of Zizzi was an occasional yes or no. The Commander sat on the edge of his chair staring at us suspiciously. His head jerked back and forth from one of us to another, and he kept tensing himself as if to spring. He may not have been a young man, but he was a wiry one. And he was armed. He could be dangerous.

Not exactly ideal conditions for diplomatic negotiations. We'd meant this first meeting to be an ice-breaker, a laying of groundwork to convince Zizzi we meant the Lodonites no harm. But we'd assumed we'd be speaking to a rational man, not this naked, wild-eyed creature gripping a spear and broadcasting hostility with every glance. He looked as if he wanted to attack us but didn't quite dare take on all six at once.

Adam spoke to him soothingly, trying to calm his fears. "The one thing we wish to avoid," he was saying, "is creating the impression that we're here to pass judgment. We're not. We're here to offer whatever assistance we can and . . ." Unflappable Adam had stopped in mid-sentence.

Commander Zizzi was masturbating.

"Oh, really," sighed Sondra. "This is too much."

I agreed. "We're going to leave now," I said to Zizzi. "We'll continue our talk later."

"Yes . . . later, later." He wanted us gone.

Outside we just stood looking helplessly at one another.

"What," said Adam, "is going on here? Has the entire planet gone berserk? How can these people fight a war? They can't even feed themselves."

We watched some neuters—I supposed they were neuters—pushing their portable soup kitchens. Another neuter worked a different area of the camp with a water bucket and a cup. Getting the drunken men and women to swallow wasn't an easy task—they tended to dribble like babies. The angry shouting of belligerent soldiers would ease off from time to time, long enough to let us hear the muttering and the snores of the more passive drunks. A terrible stench everywhere: a combination of unwashed bodies, vomit, and animal droppings.

"Why, thank you," I said aloud. "We're very glad to be here."

5

Alison had wandered away, as she often did. Ben went looking for her.

The rest of us: sitting disconsolately in a wheelless wagon at the southern edge of the Lodonite army camp. We were hot and thirsty, but the one well we'd found had been contaminated. The Whitfields hadn't even had to test the water: we could see the dead rat floating on the surface.

"Our mission may be over before it's even started," Adam was saying. "Obviously negotiations are impossible under conditions like these. Even the grand and glorious Culloden wouldn't expect us to haggle with inebriates. Those neuters did say everyone in Lodon was on a bender, didn't they? Everyone except the neuters themselves."

"Maybe we can negotiate with the neuters," I said.

"A logical possibility—and for that reason I don't trust it. I doubt that the neuters have any authority."

"They're keeping this pitiful excuse for an army alive," Justin said bitterly. Taking the army's disintegration as a personal affront?

"An army which is headed by a man," Adam pointed out, "and seems to be made up of men and women exclusively."

"Unless the neuter soldiers are all in the mountains," Justin mused.

Adam shot him a quick look. "That's a point. *These* soldiers obviously can't do any soldiering. But if the

29

neuters aren't drunk, maybe they are indeed in the mountains, fighting the good fight."

"With their commanding officer down here in the camp?" I wondered.

Sondra snorted. "That commanding officer couldn't command a dog to heel. Somebody else must be in charge in the mountains."

"Two commanding officers?" Justin frowned. "I doubt it. More likely Zizzi gave a whole series of orders to a group of field officers and then just sent them off. Mountain fighting depends on a lot of small groups with their own leaders. Ostensibly their activities are coordinated by one command center, but the individual platoons have a lot more leeway than in conventional armies. There are no pitched battles in mountain fighting, for one thing. The terrain doesn't permit it."

"So it's a guerrilla kind of fighting?" I asked.

"Just about. Skirmishes, ambushes, sniping, trap-setting. No decisive confrontations, no big dramatic events that turn the course of the war."

"Sounds like a war of attrition."

"That's exactly what it is. Keep chipping away at the other side while they keep chipping away at you, and hope *they* are debilitated before you are."

Sondra shuddered. "I think I'd rather come down out of the mountains and fight it out and get it settled once and for all."

"Whose side of the mountains would you fight it out on?" Justin smiled. "If you were a Lodonite, would you invite the Kamarian army into your country for tea and battle?" Sondra made a face at him. "No, they've probably worked out the safest way there is to fight their war. Keep it in the mountains."

Adam had a question. "Could only a third of the population—the neuters—do all the fighting for Lodon?"

"A third of the population? Certainly. More than enough. *If* that's what they're doing. We've seen some neuters down here, remember. I'd like to see what's actually going on in those mountains."

Adam nodded. "So would I. We'll go take a look tomorrow."

"Now, wait a minute—" Me, objecting.

"In the shuttle," Adam said. "We'll fly over and see what we can see. Don't worry. We're not going to be in the front line."

"There won't be any front line anyway," Justin said. "Just little pockets of fighting here and there. We'll have to scout them out."

"I can hardly wait," Sondra sighed.

Just then I had a crazy idea. "Do you suppose they take turns? Say the neuters fight while everyone else goes on a binge. Then the men fight while the neuters take some time off. And then the women give the men a rest?"

Justin's mouth dropped open. "That's crazy, Valerie. That's really crazy."

"I suppose so," I said, and gestured toward the army camp. "Especially when everything else is so *reasonable* here."

Justin threw up his hands. "*Touché.* Okay, I suppose anything's possible."

Adam, giving me one of his searching husbandly looks: "You really think that's the way they do it?"

"No," I admitted. "It just seemed dumb enough to fit in with everything else."

"Selective service by gender alone," Justin muttered. "Pay no attention to skills or training or anything else. You're a neuter? Into the cart with you. It's your month to fight."

He looked so disgruntled I had to laugh. "I withdraw the suggestion. Bad idea. Forget it."

"Here comes Ben," said Sondra. "And he's got someone with him."

We watched as Ben trudged toward us, followed by a young neuter lugging a water bucket. "This is Garrinel," Ben said, indicating his companion. "The water tests out safe."

"Garrinel, you're the best thing I've seen in hours," I said, climbing out of the wagon. The water was cool and sweet, and I drank too fast.

"Easy," said Adam.

I stepped away from the bucket and looked at the young neuter who'd brought us the water. Garrinel had a quick smile and a dimple in his (its?) chin. (I couldn't help thinking of him/it as a boy.)

"Thank you, Garrinel," said Adam when we'd all drunk. "You don't know how good that tasted. You're a life saver."

"You are welcome, mirhilancthon. If you are hungry . . . ?"

We thanked him, no. The stench of the army camp had given us all a case of the queasies. But the gesture was nice: Lodon offered what hospitality it could.

"Any sign of Alison?" I asked Ben.

"Not yet." He turned and headed back in the direction he'd come from.

"Could she have gotten lost?" Justin asked Sondra.

"Alison's always getting lost," she said, "and Ben's always finding her. Don't worry."

"Garrinel," I said, "is it true that neuters in Lodon don't drink?"

A sheepish look. "It is true, mirhiliptha."

So why that look? "Is it, Garrinel?"

A big sigh. "We are not permitted, mirhiliptha. I myself have tasted the *trang*." *Trang*—the local whiskey. "I like it. But once when I was young"—Garrinel must have been all of sixteen—"I drank too much and became *mansola*."

Mansola was a word not included in our recently acquired Lodonite vocabularies. *Mansola*, Garrinel explained when we asked, meant "safely asleep." What a euphemism for "drunk." And such a pretty-sounding word—broad *a*, stress on the first syllable. *Mansola*.

"My father found me," Garrinel went on. "He beat me. He beat me so badly I have never been *mansola* since. Nor will I ever be again."

"Good for you," I said. "Where is your father now?"

Garrinel turned and pointed. "You see the building flying the banner? That is where my father is."

The headquarters building? I exchanged a look with Adam. "Commander Zizzi is your father?"

Garrinel broke into a smile. "You know him?"

"We've met him. A couple of hours ago."

The smile disappeared. "Oh. Then you met him when he was out of *trang*." Garrinel looked embarrassed.

Take the plunge: "Garrinel, what's wrong with him?"

Garrinel's hands spread, *one of those things*. "He was out of *trang*. But I took him some. He is all right now, mirhiliptha."

I wanted to ask if Zizzi was also *mansola* now, but something in the neuter's manner held me back. Garrinel was obviously uncomfortable and soon found an opportunity to leave. We all stared after the neuter thoughtfully.

Garrinel looked like a boy, walked like a boy, spoke with a boy's voice. The only difference I could *see* between neuters and males was that the neuters had no facial hair. The male soldiers were all bearded except for those who were still too young; Zizzi's beard had been grizzled and unkempt. All the Lodonites had ruddy complexions and wore their hair either short or tied back out of the way. Men, women, and neuters all more or less dressed alike, in trousers and some variation of tunic top, made out of animal hides and thick cloth. They were a rough-looking people; even the courteous neuters we'd spoken to had an air of belligerence-held-in-restraint about them. Not unusual in a nation whose main occupation was war.

And the neuters looked like boys.

"Well?" I asked Adam. "Did Garrinel look like a girl to you?"

He nodded. "Very much so. Quite feminine."

Same thing again: Sondra said "boy," Justin said "girl."

We talked it over but could reach no conclusion other than the obvious one: there was something in the neuters that each of us recognized as being alien to us *individually*. The women sensed that Garrinel was not female and accordingly labeled him male. The men instinctively knew they were not talking to a male and so thought of Garrinel as female. The ingrained preconceptions of a bisexual race had caused us to make the wrong associations. It's not easy for Anglo-Saxon Invaders to start thinking neuter.

Waiting for the Whitfields, by Samuel Beckett. Sondra catnapping against Justin's back, her husband staring glumly over the Lodonite camp, none too thrilled with his first Corps assignment but not wanting to say so. Adam and I moved away from the wagon and sat in the shade of an ugly old tree. Vayner was directly overhead: a white star that looked runny around the edges, like the sun in a child's water-color painting. It was hot.

Un-Godotlike the Whitfields eventually showed up. Even at a distance it was clear Alison was distressed. Ben was trying to comfort her.

"She's been examining some of the soldiers," Ben explained as they sat under the tree with us.

Alison: "Have you noticed how skinny they all are? Some of them are suffering from malnutrition. None of them are really getting enough to eat. They all need vitamin infusions. If I'd just brought some supplies from the ship . . ."

I smiled at her. "You stocked enough vitamins to pep up an entire army?"

"No, of course not. But we could help some of them."

Sondra and Justin joined us under the tree. "Are we allowed to do that?" Justin asked. "Give medical aid? I thought we were supposed to avoid interfering in local conditions."

Adam shrugged. "It's one of those self-serving rules honored as much in the breach as in the observance. Technically, on evaluate-and-recommend missions we're supposed to maintain a posture of ponderous and judicial detachment, dispensing encouragement and understanding without committing ourselves to any specific course of action. But it's only a technicality. We're expected to use our own judgment."

"My judgment says we should get out of here," Sondra

remarked. "We're not going to get anywhere with this bunch."

"But this is just the army camp," I objected. "I know those neuters indicated it was like this everywhere in Lodon, but we'd better make some effort to check it out. I simply cannot conceive of an entire nation in a perpetual state of drunkenness. We ought to visit one of the villages, at least."

"Besides, it's getting to be protect-your-own-ass time," Adam agreed. "We've been here—what, about four hours? How's our report going to read? 'Everybody was drunk and it smelled bad so we left'? What we'd better do is get this place on tape. Nobody'll believe us otherwise."

"We ought to tape it anyway. For the record." Justin, the ex-historian.

With the use of the shuttle cameras, taping the Lodonite army camp would be a one-man job. We decided to split up. Adam would go back for the shuttle while the rest of us walked to a village near the camp. After Adam had his pictures, he'd fly to the village and pick us up. Too bad the tapes weren't designed to record smell as well as sight and sound.

Adam: "Where are you going? There's a village directly south of here, and another a few kilometers east."

"We'll stick with our dirty dirt road," I said. "Follow it south to the first village you come to. We'll wait there."

Adam took the food analyzer from Ben to carry back to the shuttle; none of us planned on staying to dinner. We found the road again and started out—Adam north, the rest of us south.

The road south of the camp was even more littered with debris than to the north. Within minutes we were hot and sweaty and dirty: it was early afternoon and the day's heat was at its peak. We passed a cart heading north toward the camp. The driver: sober, therefore neuter. He/it gawked at us, muttered something we couldn't understand, and urged the animal pulling the cart to try a little harder.

"I can't call a human being 'it,' " I complained.

"*I* can," Sondra muttered.

"Did you see what that cart was loaded with?" asked Ben. "Jugs. Nothing but jugs of—what's it called?"

"*Trang*," I said. "Portable potables. A kind of corn whiskey, I guess."

"Civil rebellion?" Justin asked, *à propos* of nothing that I could see.

"What civil rebellion?" Sondra.

"Could the neuters be keeping the males and females drunk as part of a concerted effort to take over the country?"

"That'd take a lot of cooperating from the men and women doing the drinking, wouldn't it?" I said.

"Yes," Justin said ruefully. "There are just so many things about this place I don't understand. I keep looking for explanations and end up guessing."

"Don't we all," Sondra murmured. "Like I find myself thinking that these people aren't really fighting a war at all. I looked at that army camp and thought it's just a joke, a bad joke they're all playing. There's no real war here. They're just playing at war as an excuse for their own bad behavior. Grossly unfair judgment, and I know it. But I keep thinking it."

Alison was quiet, keeping her thoughts to herself.

We'd been walking about half an hour when Sondra spotted smoke up ahead. As we approached, the smoke billows seemed to grow in volume more than the shortening of our perspective should allow for. We could smell it now—a stinging in the nostrils, a tickle in the throat. We all looked at one another uneasily and picked up our pace.

We jog-trotted up a small rise and confirmed what we feared: the village was on fire.

6

What we saw shocked us into temporary immobility.

What we saw: an entire row of buildings in flames.

What we saw: a group of people working feverishly to put out the fire.

What we saw: another group of people working just as feverishly at keeping it going. Feeding the fire. Laughing, playing, having a good time. Not invaders from the other side of the mountains but Lodonites—destroying their own village.

Four men and a woman running in and out of buildings not yet on fire: fetching furniture, clothing, anything that would burn. Whatever they found would go into their street-sized bonfire to the accompaniment of hysterical cheering. Somewhere: a woman shrieking. A scar-faced man performed a clumsy strip-tease in the street, tossing each piece of clothing to the fire as he took it off. Across the street an old woman had seated herself on a barrel and was cackling away as wholeheartedly as if she were watching the performance of a comedy.

The fire brigade: adults with no facial hair, passing buckets along a line from a pump in the square. Worried, sweating, doing what they could to stop the fire from spreading. Afraid of the firebugs, shrinking when one came near them, unable to stop them.

Ben Whitfield was the first to come out of his trance. A man lay drunk in a gutter dangerously near one of the burning buildings: Ben dragged him to safety and in doing so galvanized the rest of us to action. Alison and I raced to join the bucket brigade. The neuters backed away from us until I could make them understand we were there to help. The heavy buckets were hard for Alison to handle, but we freed two of the neuters to join several others trying to beat out the flames with blankets and brooms. Like the structures in the army camp, all the buildings in the village were squat, one-story affairs hugging the ground. The few made of wood went up like fireworks; most, fortunately, were built of stone.

Muscles in my arms and back were beginning to protest when I looked up to see Sondra make a flying tackle of the woman who was part of the gang of arsonists. Justin went to Sondra's aid; I was alarmed to see he had blood on his face. The two of them wrestled the woman—who seemed extraordinarily strong—down the street to what looked like some sort of animal cage. The other four firebugs were crouching inside; Ben unbarred the cage and shoved the woman in with her companions. How do you react when a stranger locks you in a cage? Well, *these* five were shrieking and laughing as if it were all some marvelous joke. Sondra and the two men came hurrying over to join the bucket brigade.

Without the firebugs to feed the flames, we started to get things under control. First one building, then another died down. No new fires broke out. We were wetting down adjacent buildings just to be on the safe side when I noticed all the neuters had disappeared. The old woman on the barrel sat cackling at our efforts.

The firebugs had fallen silent, except for one man who would occasionally give a deep, gulping sob. Justin poured one last bucket of water over some still-smoldering timbers. We stood in the street and looked around us, wondering whether everyone on this planet was stark, raving mad.

One entire side of the street was burned, and two buildings on the other side. They were small buildings: I couldn't tell if they'd been shops or homes. The five of us were covered with smoke, sweat, and dirt; Justin wore the added adornment of dried blood from a scalp wound he'd picked up wrestling with the firebugs.

"I wonder whether they were all empty," Sondra said glumly, staring at the smoke-streaked facade of one of the buildings.

The old woman on the barrel let loose a cackle that would have made a witch proud; she was beginning to get on my nerves. "Look," I said to the others, "I don't know about you, but I've had it for today. Let's find some place away from this mess and just hole up until Adam gets here with the shuttle."

They all muttered agreement. We turned our backs on the burnt-out street and trudged away; I felt as if I'd walked a hundred kilometers since breakfast.

Once out of earshot of the cackling old woman: silence, a tangible silence—unbroken and oppressive. The village seemed deserted. Where had the fire-fighting neuters gone? Where were the men and women? The animals? Nothing: no sign of life anywhere. Doors stood open, as if the buildings had been hastily abandoned by their occupants. Which they probably had been, if there'd been anyone around with sense enough to flee.

And what about children? I realized I hadn't seen a child since we touched down on this planet. We couldn't expect to find them in the army camp—but an entire village without children?

Before we knew it we found ourselves back on our dirty dirt road facing south again: it had taken us only ten minutes to walk all the way through the village. Nothing to do but turn back. We did—and saw the missing villagers.

They were dancing.

There must have been nearly fifty of them, dancing in the village's main street to a music only they could hear. This was no dance of celebration; nor was it a stylized ritual mourning. The dancers all performed the same steps, but no two performed in unison. Movements were jerky, uncoordinated, unbeautiful. Elbows out, heads back, knees pumping up and down. And not a single sound except that of feet slapping the hard ground. *Not even the sound of breathing.* It was an eerie, surrealistic performance that made me hold my own breath as I watched.

We moved in closer and saw: flecks of foam on the dancers' mouths. One man swinging his head back and forth rapidly, spraying foam on the other dancers. They didn't notice.

Their absolute silence made my flesh crawl—high-pumping knees, wildly jerking elbows, and no sound except feet going slap-slap-slap. The dancers' unfocused eyes looked right through us: we could have been invisible. Once we had to move quickly to keep from being trampled. They didn't notice.

One man twitched spastically and his elbow shot out to catch a woman dancer in the eye. She didn't notice.

Another man flung out a hand and hit a smaller man square in the face. The smaller man's lip began to bleed. He didn't notice.

Fifty thin, unseeing, "possessed" men and women, jerking arhythmically as if controlled by some amateur puppeteer. As unnatural as it was, this grotesque procession didn't seem totally unfamiliar. Something teased at my memory. I'd read of this, or . . . We watched the whole group lurch its way around a corner in total silence, and then it came to me.

"Dancing mania," I said. "During Earth's middle ages—what caused it, Alison?"

"Ergotism," she said promptly. "And you're right. It looks just like it."

"What?" Justin, still a little dazed by the dancers.

"Ergotism. An affliction caused by eating bread made from ergot-infested rye," Alison explained. "One of the chemical compounds of ergot is D-lysergic acid amide."

"An LSD trip?" Sondra, incredulous.

"Yep. One in which the entire community participated. Unwillingly, and unknowingly."

"Any way we can find out?" I asked.

Ben: "If we can get a couple of those dancers back to the ship, Alison and I can run some tests. The presence of ergot is easily detected—maybe Lodon has its own version of the fungus. We'll pick up the dancers as soon as Adam gets here with the shuttle."

"Where *is* Adam?" asked Sondra. "What's taking him so long?"

Justin: "Could something have happened to him?"

"Unlikely," I said. "Something may have held him up, but he'll get here." I didn't see any point in saying so, but Adam could take care of himself better than any of us.

"You don't seem very worried about your husband," Justin snapped.

"Sorry," I said calmly. "How worried would you like me to be?"

Sondra watched us both with detachment, keeping out of it.

Justin immediately regretted his show of nerves. "It's this place—it's beginning to get to me, I guess."

Suddenly I felt sorry for him. He'd had a lot to cope with all at once: a new marriage, a new profession, a new group of co-workers who'd all known one another for years. And a "new" planet as well, one that seemed to worship the god of chaos. Lodon was a handful even for us experienced types; no neophyte should have been sent here.

I patted him on the arm. "I think you're handling it all beautifully, Justin. Just hang on a little longer—we'll be back in the ship soon." And then could have bitten my tongue: I sounded so damned condescending.

But Sondra nodded: *that's all right, then.*

Just then the dancers lurched back into view— pumping, flapping, seemingly not breathing. They crossed the main thoroughfare where we were standing and were soon out of sight. All except one woman. Somehow separated from her companions, she danced her solo down the street away from us.

Like a piece of machinery in need of lubrication: moving in fits and starts. She'd slap a foot on the ground and pose a second or two with her other knee shoulder-high. Then slap and pose: change feet. Balanced on one foot, with her crooked arms flapping and her long nose pointed toward the sky, she looked like some enormous wading bird on the verge of taking flight.

"Where's Alison?" said Ben. "Al?"

"Over here." Alison was leaning out the window of a small cottage. "We can stay here. It's . . ."

She trailed off as we became aware of some kind of racket behind us. We were still at the southern edge of the village; coming up the dirt road from the south was a group of raucous, shrieking men and women. Not dancers: more like the crazed arsonists we'd encountered earlier.

"Inside," I said. "We don't want to tangle with that bunch." We all hurried to Alison's cottage and barred the door. The cottage had two rooms—the first was a leather-working shop; the back room, living quarters. We left the shutters of the front window open a trifle so we could see what was happening outside.

Justin: "How will Adam know where we are?"

"Don't worry, he'll find us," I said. Adam's instincts were good. As a pilot he was the one who controlled movement; he had a sense of direction a homing pigeon would have envied. He'd find us.

They came roaring into the village like avenging furies bent on punishing the collective sins of all mankind. Shrieking, wild-eyed creatures, filled with hate and the urge to destroy. These Lodonites were breakers, not burners; they set about smashing everything in sight.

We stood anxiously in the semi-dark shop listening to the splintering of wood and the smashing of crockery, all to the accompaniment of hysterical giggles and roaring-animal belly laughs. I peeked through the shutters and saw a man with a heavy hammer enter a cottage across the way and start breaking up whatever he found there. Through the open door of the other cottage I could see the hammer—rising and falling, rising and falling.

Eventually the hammer-wielder saw something he didn't want to break and came out carrying three or four jugs. Which he passed around real friendly-like. When the jugs were empty, several of the rioters staggered away, looking for more.

Now I was worried about Adam. He'd have no idea what was going on here. He'd put the shuttle down near the village and meander in not suspecting a thing. No— no, he wouldn't: Adam wasn't careless. Especially not on a strange planet. And this was a *strange* planet. Adam didn't make impulsive moves; he'd be all right.

Still . . .

Someone tried to break into our shop. I hastily closed the window shutters and slipped the bar into its holders; whoever was trying to break in soon gave up and went on somewhere else. Laughing. The most frightening thing about the ravaging of the village was the lunatic glee with which it was carried out. Screeching unmotivated laughter, shouts of improbable joy, happy destructive hate-filled people at play. Great community spirit here in Lodon.

Then: a high, terrified scream that made me skip a heartbeat. Repeated: not part of the general racket made by the destructive revelers, definitely not part of it. And once again: It was a young girl's scream.

We fell over each other trying to get through the door. Four men had a girl barely in her teens down on her back in the street. She was shrieking and gasping, beating with small fists at the shaggy, half-naked man who'd mounted her.

Justin was the first to reach them. He lunged: only to meet two hard fists in his face. I saw him fall to the ground, the lower half of his face covered with blood. Alison and I grabbed the girl's arms while Ben and Sondra struggled with the man on top of her. We managed to pull the girl away and get her to her feet.

She thanked us by kicking us.

Surprised: Alison and I let loose. The girl flopped back down in the street. Automatically we reached for her again.

"Get away!" the girl spat at us. "Get away!"

We hesitated. And in that moment of hesitation we lost whatever advantage we might have gained. Ben: trying to protect himself from three of the angered rapists. Four or five women from out of nowhere running at us, flailing their arms, screaming. Justin, rolling over just in time to avoid a kick in the groin. The hammer-wielder and his drinking buddies were back—with reinforcements. Who—for no reason—began fighting with the rapists. *Not* taking our side, not trying to protect us. Just fighting for the pleasure of fighting: any old opponent would do. We were caught in a sinister free-for-all that was attracting more and more of these lunatics.

I was yelling to the others to run when one of the Lodonite men grabbed me in a tight embrace: he reeked of urine and *trang*. He forced me down to my knees and was bending me backward; I pulled back my hand and hit him in the nostrils with the butt of my palm as hard as I could. *Danger, danger*: a splinter of bone could penetrate the brain and cause immediate death.

The man gave a roar of pain and clutched at his broken nose. One of the drunken fighters careened into him and we all three went down. Broken Nose was howling and dripping blood and mucus on me: not very dead. Sondra and Alison: tugging at the two Lodonites, rolling them away, helping me up.

We retreated.

Sondra hauled her bleeding husband to his feet and we all staggered back to our leatherworker's shop. Justin had multiple cuts around his mouth and had lost a tooth. Alison had a nasty scratch down one cheek. Ben's left thumb was broken. Sondra and I got off with a few minor bumps and bruises.

We sat in the shop without talking, waiting for Adam and the shuttle, each of us wrapped in a private little cocoon of fear. There were other screams. We ignored them.

The only light in the shop came from a chink where the wooden window shutters didn't quite meet. I sat against the wall under the window and watched the dust motes dancing in the thin streak of sunlight over my head. My right thigh began to feel cramped: I was half sitting on something.

A loose tangle of leather straps connected in some way

I couldn't immediately make out. Metal studs. A few buckles. It was a harness. The leather was smooth and evenly cut and smelled new. Fingering it gave me a kind of reassurance: the harness had been put together by someone who took pride in his work.

What was this—a flaw? My finger ran over a rough spot in the leather. It didn't feel like a defect in the leather: it was too regular. I stood up and held the harness to the light.

Sondra: "What is it, Val?"

"A bird," I said. "Somebody's tooled a tiny line drawing of a bird on this harness." So. The artistic impulse, the need to impose order on chaos—it managed to survive even madhouse conditions like these.

The brawlers and rioters had moved off. We could hear them not far away, their desperate laughter ringing through the streets. Still we stayed in our shop.

"Valerie? Valerie?" Adam's voice, faint. At last: It seemed like hours.

"Here, Adam!" I hoisted up the bar from the door and stepped out into the now deserted street.

Adam took one look at me and his mouth twisted in distress. He ran over and grabbed me by the arms: I looked down and saw I was covered with Broken Nose's blood.

"It's all right, I'm not hurt," I told Adam hastily. "It's not my blood."

"You should see the other guy," Sondra said grimly. "Where's the shuttle?"

"Just east of the village. But what happened?"

"Tell you later," I said. "Right now we need to get a couple of those dancers. For medical tests. And then let's get out of here."

Adam: "There's a whole gang of them a few streets from here. What an insane place! I've been playing hide-and-seek for the last half-hour, trying to find you. Let's go."

Justin had earlier questioned the ethics of interfering with local conditions on an alien planet by introducing unauthorized medical aid. Now he didn't bat an eye when we virtually kidnapped two citizens of our host country. The dancers offered no resistance; they had no understanding of what was happening. We took one man and one woman, and they let us lead them away like children. A touch of irony: we wouldn't have been able to take the dancers with us in one trip if the Corps had provided the smaller shuttles we'd asked for. The brief flight back to the JX-31 was grim and silent, broken only once when one of the dancers burst out babbling for a moment, then lapsed back into silence.

Home: back on board ship.

"Do you realize," Sondra said, "that girl we tried to rescue is the youngest person we've seen since we got here?"

"Where are the children?" I nodded.

Ben: "Children couldn't survive down there on their own. I don't understand how even the adults have managed to survive—even with the neuters feeding them and putting out their fires. A small child wouldn't stand a chance in a place like that."

"Either they're shut away someplace where they can't be hurt or can't hurt themselves," Sondra said, "or they haven't survived."

Horrible statement of the obvious: a land with no children is a land with no future.

Alison treated Justin's bleeding socket and promised him a temporary tooth as soon as his gum tissue had healed. She set Ben's thumb and tended to her own scratched face. Then she and Ben took the two dancers into the laboratory and started their tests.

The rest of us retired to our cabins; it was with great relief that Adam and I at last shut our door against the stresses of the day. I was keyed up and edgy; Adam came through with the oldest cure for jitters known to man. But I couldn't get images of Lodon out of my head; I lay awake a long time, soaking up the warmth generated by Adam's sleeping body.

On the brink of sleep I realized I was nursing an almost childish hope that the Whitfields would come up with some explanation, some magic solution that would

let us do the job we'd been sent here to do. If there were
a medical reason behind the Lodonites' insane behavior,
then all we had to do was analyze it and find a cure,
right?

Kiss it and make it well.

7

"No ergotism."

We were gathered in the wardroom the next morning eating breakfast when Alison and Ben told us the first test results.

"Strange blood, though," said Alison. "Thingummy in there we can't identify. We'll need some time."

Sondra Bark was our behavioral expert, so I asked her if she'd seen any individual crazies in Lodon.

"What do you mean?"

"I mean anybody who was acting crazy in a way that was different from the way everybody else was acting crazy."

"No, they all came in groups—the drunks, the burners, the breakers, the dancers. Even Commander Zizzi was showing the same kind of hostility some of his soldiers were showing—the ones who weren't flat-on-their-backs drunk."

"Do you think it could be mass hysteria?"

"Only if an organic basis for their behavior can be ruled out. I'd want to know what Alison's thingummy is before I say."

"Clinically, *could* it be mass hysteria?"

"Clinically, yes. It has all the earmarks."

"Then we should consider that possibility while Alison and Ben try to track down an organic basis. If it is mass hysteria, something had to trigger it."

Justin: "Unless that's just the way they are. Is it possible that what we saw yesterday is typical of Lodonite life? Could that madness be permanent?"

Adam shook his head. "Don't see how it could be. Somebody constructed those buildings, somebody made their clothes, grew the food they eat. Even if all the neuters are sober and sane—and we don't really know they are, remember—but if they are, they still couldn't manage to do all the work necessary to keep the other two-thirds of the population going. A belligerent two-thirds, at that. No, that bedlam can't be a permanent state of affairs. There has to be some other explanation."

Ben wiped up some coffee he'd spilled. "Alison and I are fairly certain it's a disease that's causing the trouble. Of epidemic proportions, to judge from what we saw yesterday. That substance we found in the dancers' blood— we don't know what it is or what it does. It may have nothing at all to do with disease—but we'd better find out. It'll take us a while, but that's *our* next step."

I nodded. "And ours, I suppose, is a trip to the mountains. There's no point in going back to the army camp that I can see. Adam, better tell them about Zizzi."

"I stopped back at the headquarters building after we separated yesterday," Adam said. "Zizzi was stretched out on a straw mattress, sleepy-drunk. There was one empty jug on the floor, and another one about half full. Zizzi'd been covered with a blanket and there was food in his beard, so someone had been by to take care of him. Probably Garrinel—Zizzi's neuter offspring, the one who gave us the water?"

The others nodded.

"Anyway, Zizzi mistook me for someone else—kept calling me something that sounded like 'Bithor.' And he insisted I *sing* to him. Really insisted. He started to get worked up about it, so I sat down by his mattress and began making up Lodonite words to any tune I could think of. The fact that the songs made no sense didn't matter to Zizzi. He lay there peacefully, nodding in time to the music until he drifted off. So all the time you were putting out the fire in the village, I was holding that old man's hand and singing him to sleep. Zizzi's out of it now, completely out of it. Val's right—there's no point in going back to the army camp."

"What about the dancers?" I asked the Whitfields. "Are you finished with them?"

"You can take them back," Ben said. "We took small samples of their body fluids—we were afraid to take much, they're so undernourished."

Justin shot a curious glance at Alison. "Did you . . . ?"

"I certainly did," she smiled. "Those two Lodonites, at least, are vitamin-enriched."

"Good," said Justin. Positively.

The Whitfields went back to their lab while the rest of us steered the dancers into the shuttle. They were in a kind of stupor which seemed to be the dancers' equivalent of sleep. The woman had a long strip of plastiflesh applied to her left forearm—closing a gash the Whitfields had treated, I supposed.

Adam touched down just north of the ravaged village. Sondra and Justin roused the two dancers and pointed them south. We watched them dance away, wondering if they would survive what we were sending them back to.

Then: off to war.

The shuttle scanners weren't as powerful as those in the JX-31, so Adam had to fly close in if we were to get a good look. The mountain terrain was unusual: very few soaring peaks towering over the rest of the world, mostly jagged upthrusts of land and rock in an almost helter-skelter pattern. And it was lovely. Wild and hushed and not too far removed in time from the moment of creation. Even up close the montane forests had a bluish cast to them, enhanced and softened by fingers of mist that felt their way through the gorges and the valleys. The place looked as if it were waiting for something.

I was so taken with the beauty of the mountains I almost forgot what I was supposed to be watching out for. "Anybody see an army?" Nobody had.

And that was the trouble. After three hours we still hadn't spotted a single living soul in the mountains.

Sondra, irritated: "I knew it. They aren't really fighting a war at all. They're just pretending to fight."

"Mind if I give it a try?" Justin asked Adam. The two men changed places and Justin began to follow the terrain in a pattern I couldn't figure out. Then before too much more time had passed we caught sight of a small squad of soldiers, only six or seven of them. They seemed to be rigging some sort of catapult in a narrow pass between two outcroppings of rock. Since our shuttle didn't have hover capabilities, we had to content ourselves with a slow pass overhead. The minute the soldiers saw us coming they scattered and disappeared.

"They probably think the Kamarians have come up with a new secret weapon," I said.

"Those *were* Kamarians," said Justin. "Did you see which way that catapult was aimed? Eastward, toward Lodon. I wonder if they leave a man behind to trigger it or depend upon a careless enemy foot to do the job."

We saw nothing else the rest of the day. We scouted the range for two more days; and as Justin became more adept at seeking out likely places in the mountains, we began to spot pockets of soldiers quite often. Most of them were digging, building, working on something. We learned that the Lodonites and the Kamarians rarely engaged in hand-to-hand combat. Their method of waging war consisted almost entirely of building booby traps for each other. Traps for boobies; how fitting. Some of the traps were simple, such as camouflaged pits planted with sharpened staves. Others were more elaborate, such as the catapults of the sort we'd seen the first day.

By zigzagging we were able to follow one platoon of soldiers who plodded on like well-herded cattle, determinedly ignoring the strange-looking thing flying over their heads. They led us to a fast-moving mountain stream spanned by a rickety-looking wooden bridge. It took the soldiers about ten minutes to set fire to the bridge and then disappear into the landscape. Yellow flames licked at the wooden structure as smoke billowed upward. No fire brigade appeared to stop the damage.

"Interesting," said Justin. "No gunpowder, no explosives of any kind. Yet their entire orientation is toward long-distance weaponry. Catapults, traps. Bridge-burning when the enemy isn't in the neighborhood. And as well as I could tell, those soldiers were carrying more slings than they were close-fighting weapons like knives or axes. Almost as if they're trying to avoid grappling with the enemy in person."

Toward the end of the day we saw one group of fourteen Kamarians unknowingly trip a complicated rope-and-lever system which precipitated a landslide that buried all fourteen of them. We kept circling the place long after it was clear there were no survivors, all four of us in a state of shock: it had happened so quickly. It was a clear victory for Lodon, but there wasn't a Lodonite anywhere to witness it.

It was war, and in war people die. You can tell yourself that until you're blue in the face, but it still doesn't cushion you against the fact when it happens right under your nose.

Adam broke the tension by saying, "I don't know whether my imagination's running away with me or not, but it seems to me the Kamarians outnumber the Lodonites by about two to one. Does that seem right to you, Justin?"

"Just about."

"Are the Kamarians winning?"

"I'd say it was about even. Neither side has gained much advantage that I can see."

"The Kamarians have twice as many soldiers as the Lodonites," Adam mused, "and they're fighting a country that's in the grip of some sort of epidemic. And yet they don't seem to be making any real progress. Extraordinary."

Nobody had any heart for what we were doing, so Justin took the shuttle back to the JX-31. Ben Whitfield was waiting at the end of the crawl chute.

"See anything interesting?" he wanted to know.

"We saw fourteen people die," Sondra told him.

Ben shot her a look and then said quickly, "Come to the wardroom in about half an hour. I've got something to show you." Giving us time to unwind.

When we gathered in the wardroom a little later, Ben

had set up a microprojection for our benefit. It showed a vivid mustard-colored network of cells with Siamese nuclei and organelle populations so thick as to appear almost solid. Thousands of lacy cilia waved gracefully; whatever this thing was, it could move.

Ben: "Alison's still in the lab, but we thought one of us ought to bring you up to date on what we've found so far. The Lodonite blood contains a substance unfamiliar to us. You're looking at it now. Pretty, isn't it? Call it Substance X. It has a chemical structure resembling that of adrenalin, but there seems to be a disproportionately high amount of it in the dancers' blood."

I asked, "Disproportionately high as measured against what?"

"As measured against the amount of adrenalin the human body normally releases in high-stress situations, that is to say, the most released *ever*. Without a full laboratory and more specialized testing equipment than we have here we can't be absolutely sure, but what we think happens is this. Substance X seems to do two things. First, it stimulates the sensory cortex. Second, it releases transmitter chemicals at the synapses between sympathetic neurons and the tissues which they inervate. That would account for the dancers' jerky, uncontrolled movements."

"It would account for a couple of other things as well," said Sondra. "Hostility, for one."

"Yes!" Ben exclaimed. "We think Substance X acts something like an overdose of one of the amphetamines. We kept our two dancers under restraints for a period before testing them—to rest them, to calm them down. But they still showed a superfast heart rate and high blood pressure. And high blood sugar. Alison thinks they were hallucinating as well."

Sondra: "That's probably why Commander Zizzi acted as if he didn't trust us. Chronic amphetamine users sometimes react with extreme suspicion toward everything and everyone around them. Or they tend toward aggressive, assaultive behavior—they want to take physical action quickly, without regard for the consequences. Like those people we tangled with in the village."

"But what about the soldiers in the army camp?" I wondered. "Their behavior was nothing like that of the villagers. Their lassitude, their indifference—"

"They were intoxicated, Val," said Ben. "In their sober state they probably behave exactly like the others. *If* they have the disease. Don't forget alcohol is a depressant."

Adam: "Remember the Lodonite word for 'drunk'? *Mansola.* 'Safely asleep.' Pretty accurate description under the circumstances. When they're drunk, they don't hurt anybody. Not even themselves."

"All right," I said. "Then tell me this: How did Substance X get into their bodies in the first place? Is it hereditary?"

"Doubt it," said Ben. "Its effects are so violent that the race would have killed itself off long ago if this were a permanent condition. It was probably ingested."

So Adam had been right. "The effects will eventually wear off, then."

"That's the ugly part," Ben said slowly. "I said Substance X had a chemical structure resembling that of adrenalin—resembling, not identical to. When adrenalin has finished its job of stimulating the liver or relaxing the bronchioles or rerouting the blood or whatever else it might be doing, it breaks down into simpler components that just pass out of the body. And here's the difference: Substance X doesn't break down."

"There's no way to break it down artificially?" Adam.

"That's what Alison's working on now. We're trying everything we can think of. But so far, nothing. That means we can't concoct a vaccine—we need *killed* organisms to put into a suspension."

We all fell silent, thinking over the implications of what Ben had said. If the Lodonites had a disease that couldn't be counted on to run its course, eventually the entire male and female population would die out. Starvation and bodily injury would account for large numbers of them; the neuters couldn't take care of all of them forever. And if the males and females died out, eventually so would the neuters. Who would give birth to them?

The eventual demise of the entire nation of Lodon

would leave the Kamarians in sole possession of the planet. That would make our own course of action quite clear: negotiate mining rights with the Kamarians and then get the hell out of here. The Culloden would approve, no question of that. Trouble was, *I* didn't approve.

Our initial feeling of disgust at the way the Lodonite army camp was run had disappeared as soon as we learned these people were ill. It would be so easy for us to exploit their weakness to fulfill our assignment, so easy for us to make ourselves look good at the Lodonites' expense.

But how do you turn your back on a dying nation? And what do you do if you *don't* turn your back? Even if the Whitfields did find a way of breaking down Substance X, what then? Ben and Alison were on our team as medical observers and to treat any member of the team who might fall ill. Their shipboard lab wasn't set up to handle an epidemic.

"Ben," I asked, "if you and Alison do find a way to break down Substance X, will someone who's had the disease then be immune?"

"I don't know," he said simply. "You're wondering whether we can stop the disease, aren't you? I think you'd better assume we can't. It's just too big a job for six people working out of a minimally equipped laboratory. You'd need a complete pathology team for that."

We all looked at each other disconsolately. All except Justin—to whom all things were still possible. "Well, *send* for one then!" he said indignantly. "If it's going to take a pathology team to save these people, then signal Corps Headquarters—"

"We could do that," I interrupted him. "We're here, and we see what it's like, and we know what should be done. But Culloden might not see it that way. In fact, you can be damned sure he won't."

Justin was incredulous, not understanding. "You're going to have to explain that to me."

Adam took over. "It's like this, Justin. Culloden wants to reach an agreement about mining rights with the people of this planet. The primary obstacle is the war—as you know, the alphidium deposits are located right where the Lodonites and the Kamarians do their own peculiar kind of fighting. Now what would happen if Culloden sent in a pathology team? Say they did find a cure for the disease and the Lodonites are restored to health. What next? Why, the war would continue, with both sides at full strength. And we'd be no closer to a mining agreement than we were before we sent for the pathology team."

Justin: "You mean Culloden would let all these people die just to get the alphidium? He'd refuse to send in pathologists just because—"

"Oh, he wouldn't outright refuse," Adam said. "He's far too subtle for that. He'd shake his head and murmur, 'Those poor people,' and juggle schedules and invent delays and make exquisitely phrased excuses until we got the message: no agreement, no pathology team. The way things stand now, the only way we're going to get help for the Lodonites is to stand on their necks while we work out something with the Kamarians."

"I don't believe it," Justin said bluntly.

"Believe it," said Sondra. "Justin, I tried to warn you before we started what kind of man Culloden is. The rest of us have worked under him for eleven years, and we've seen him pull this kind of stunt time and again. I think the Lodonites are doomed no matter what happens. Either they die out from this disease, or they're going to be subjugated by the Kamarians—with a little help from the Federation. That would be better than dying, of course. But it's a hell of a solution."

Ben cleared his throat. "You're all assuming something we don't know to be true. We don't know the Kamarians are healthy."

We all stared at him.

"This disease may be *pan*demic," he went on. "It may be confined to the Lodonite side of the mountains, but then again it may not. If the disease is global, we've got a whole new set of problems. We've got to find out if the Kamarians are disease-free or not. But before we do that, there's one other thing. I've been looking for a gentle way to say this, but here goes. Have you all overlooked the fact that you might be carriers? Or even that you may be infected yourselves?"

Adam and I exchanged a glance; we had indeed overlooked it.

Ben: "Maybe we weren't in Lodon long enough to pick up the disease, but since we know so little about it we can't assume that we're 'clean.' Alison and I have already checked our own blood—no Substance X. But before we contact the Kamarians, I want to make sure your blood is clean too. And there's no time like the present. Val, you're first. Come along."

I followed him into the lab and waited while he tested my blood. Alison didn't even look up from her work. When Ben said okay, I went back to the wardroom and sent Adam in.

We were all clean.

"Maybe offworlders are immune," Sondra suggested.

"Maybe," Ben said noncommittally.

Tomorrow we would take the shuttle and fly low over a few Kamarian villages and *their* army camp. The scanners would tell us if the Kamarians were acting like the Lodonites or whether they seemed to be normal. Ben had given us two bad shocks in quick succession. None of us had allowed ourselves to think that we too might become raving maniacs like those pitiful people we'd seen in Lodon. Nor were we ready to deal with the possibility of an entire planet full of madmen.

What happened next depended on Kamaria. We all went to sleep that night wondering what it would be like on the western side of the mountains.

8

It was like leaving the nightmare landscapes of Hieronymus Bosch for the ordered world of Jan Vermeer.

Our flyby had shown us peaceful, industrious villages and an orderly, disciplined army camp. We kept the shuttle cameras running, taping everything we saw. And what we saw was that the disease had not crossed the mountains: we'd be dealing with rational people once again. We'd put down just west of the camp, and were now standing outside the shuttle waiting for our welcoming committee.

There's always some tension in a first contact, but right now it was all I could do to keep from grinning like an idiot. Kamaria was healthy! Advancing toward us: a stolid, we-know-what-we're-doing group of soldiers. Cautious, curious, in control. Armed. They'd be fools not to come armed; they didn't know who we were or what we wanted.

Out in front: the commander, obviously. The man had "leader" written all over him. We knew his name was Fluth, but that was all we knew about him. Dark complexion, hair loose but not very long, clean-shaven. Square-built, authoritative in his walk and mien. About fifty years old. At least he looked fifty: warlike people usually seem older than they really are. At any rate, Fluth appeared to be at least twenty years younger than his Lodonite counterpart, Commander Zizzi. One startling incongruity: on Commander Fluth's shoulder perched a bird—about the size of an English woodcock, an eye-catching golden color.

They approached to within ten meters of us and stopped, waiting. It was up to us to make the first move. I stepped forward and said, "Commander Fluth? My name is Valerie Chester. We are from the Federation of United Worlds. With your permission, we would like to visit Kamaria."

The Commander looked me over carefully. "Why?" he asked bluntly.

Because you've got something we want. "Do you object to our visit?" I temporized.

"I want to know why," he insisted.

All right, if it's blunt talk you want. "We want to talk to you about joining the Federation."

"What if we don't want to join the Federation?"

"Then that's one of the things we'll talk about."

A corner of his mouth twitched. "Why don't you go talk to the Lodonites?"

"Because we're in Kamaria."

He gave a mirthless laugh and spit on the ground. "Lodonites! Deal with them, and you'll not deal with us! Show me your weapons," he commanded abruptly.

"We carry none," I said limply. "We pose no danger to you, Commander. We don't threaten you. We may even be able to help you. All we want to do is *talk.*"

Adam stepped up next to me and said, "Commander Fluth, we know we're intruding here, and for that we apologize. If you wish us to leave, we will. But we hope you'll invite us to stay. We think it's time your world and ours got acquainted."

The Commander said nothing to this but gave Adam the same kind of scrutiny he'd given me earlier. "Who are you?"

"I'm Adam Chester."

Fluth glanced at me. "Chester? You have the same name?"

No marriage ceremony on Lodon-Kamaria, I remembered. "In our culture," I explained, "when a man and a woman accept each other as mates, they take the same last name."

Commander Fluth grunted. "What does that make easier?"

His question took me by surprise, and I laughed. "Why, nothing really, I suppose. It's simply a custom of long standing."

And with that, the Commander relaxed a little. We were not infallible beings come to take over his world after all. We were just people. "What do you want to do in Kamaria?"

Adam too decided blunt talk was best. "Mostly we want to sell *you* on the idea of joining the Federation. We figure if we can convince you, your countrymen will follow your lead."

Fluth allowed his eyes to smile but kept his mouth straight. "And why should I agree?"

"Aha!" Adam raised an expository finger. "We have numerous arguments of varying degrees of persuasiveness we are willing to trot out for your personal inspection. But there's only one real reason—we think it will be mutually advantageous. Could we talk about it? Would you permit us to visit your camp?"

The Commander stared at Adam a long time and then made up his mind. "You can stay," he said roughly, and then pointed a finger at Adam. "But no weapons, mirhilancthon Chester. Or you either, mirhiliptha," to me.

"Wouldn't dream of it," I said. "Now meet our friends, Commander, none of whom carry weapons either."

I introduced him first to the Whitfields and then to the Barks. When he came to Justin, Commander Fluth said, "Welcome, mirhilaves."

Mirhilaves. The Lodonite-Kamarian term for addressing a neuter.

"This is mirhilancthon Justin Bark," Adam said smoothly, "the mate of mirhiliptha Sondra Bark."

But he wasn't smooth enough. A strange thing happened: Commander Fluth and his soldiers looked first shocked, and then embarrassed. Fluth's dark face darkened even further, and he muttered what sounded like an apology. Then he told us we could visit the army camp and whirled about and strode away before we could give him an answer. Fluth's abrupt movement caused the golden bird on his shoulder to take flight. The soldiers avoided looking at us and tramped away after their leader.

"What in the world do you make of that?" Adam asked. "Why would Justin's being a male instead of neuter cause all that to-do?"

Justin: "Fluth was acting as if he'd made a fool of himself in front of his men and that it was my fault. What did I do? *I'm* the one who should feel insulted!"

I shivered. "The early scouting reports said the Kamarians and the Lodonites were hostile only toward each other. To offworlders, they're supposed to be indifferent. Would you call that indifferent?"

"Yes," Sondra said promptly. "Did you see how Commander Fluth wheeled around and stalked away once he'd decided we were harmless?"

"*That's* not why he stalked away," said Justin grimly.

Up ahead: Commander Fluth stopping, giving orders to two of his soldiers who started walking back toward us.

"Our escort?" Alison.

The two soldiers stopped a few meters away, planted the butt ends of their spears in the ground, and stared.

"Our guard." Adam.

"The Commander did invite us to visit the camp, didn't he?" I said to the soldiers.

"Yes, mirhiliptha. Do you want to go now?" The words were courteous but the tone was guarded. These two spear carriers were both men—rough-looking no-nonsense types. One of them had an eye missing. Suddenly a golden bird—the same one? a pet?—flew up and perched on the shoulder of the one-eyed man. Absently he raised one rough hand and stroked the golden feathers.

We followed our guards to the camp and allowed ourselves to yield to a moment of exhilaration. This was a real army camp, the antithesis of that military parody we'd seen in Lodon. Rows of well-maintained permanent buildings, equipment in good repair, animals well tended.

Sane, sober soldiers going about their business. We were back in contact with the familiar, the civilized, the *touchable*. There was a reality about Kamaria that was totally missing in Lodon—Ben's broken thumb and Justin's tooth notwithstanding. That was transitory; this was permanent.

And the birds! All over the camp, the same species of golden bird as the one riding the one-eyed guard's shoulder. Clearly unafraid of people, they perched everywhere—on shoulders, in laps, on the backs of pack animals, on rooftops. Unexpected, yes; but somehow still a vital part of the picture.

Suddenly I felt a light touch in my hair and a tickling against my scalp.

"You've got a bird on your head," Ben told me.

I put my hand to my hair and felt small claws wrap themselves around my fingers. I lifted my hand to in front of my face, and gazed at the golden bird I was holding. It was a delicate, lovely creature that let me stroke its back. Just then another bird flew to Alison's shoulder and nestled against her cheek.

"What do you call them?" I asked our one-eyed guard.

"Bibblings," he said.

Soon each member of the team had his/her own bibbling. The birds were gentle and clean. They did not object to the touch of the human hand, and their feathers were like velvet. My bibbling hopped to my shoulder, and we all set out to tour the camp.

Justin Bark: the object of considerable feminine attention. A lot of friendly glances came dancing his way, as well as a tentative smile or two. One woman, bolder than the rest, started walking toward us with the clear intention of speaking to Justin. But when she got to within a few meters, a puzzled look came over her face and she stopped. Then without saying a word she turned and walked away again.

Sondra, wryly. "Maybe it's your deodorant."

The Kamarians were repairing equipment, checking food supplies, making new weapons. They all worked quietly, efficiently, with a sense of urgency—as if some deadline were drawing near. A corduroy timber road had been laid down; over it rolled small solid-wheel carts carrying paraphernalia for building traps in the mountains.

"That road," said Justin. "See how it runs well up into the mountain?"

"Yes," I said.

"The Lodonites have no roads like that. The terrain on their side of the range is much rougher. It's probably not possible to build a road from the camp—or at any of the combat access points we saw. The Kamarians cannot only get their fighting equipment up to the mountains faster, they can also keep their supply trains moving steadily."

I began to see what he was getting at.

"The Kamarians are so obviously better organized and more efficient it's hardly worth mentioning," Justin went on. "And there's no sickness here. Also, remember the Kamarians seem to have about twice as many soldiers in the mountains as the Lodonites do."

"So why haven't the Kamarians won the war."

"Exactly."

I had no answer. No answers to a lot of things. We stopped to watch two "soldiers," a boy and a girl who couldn't be more than ten years old, perform a rather unpleasant task. They were pressing a milky liquid out of small shiny-dark leaves. When I asked, the girl told me the liquid was poisonous. A dangerous job for such small hands, but the children's movements were deft and sure.

When they had collected a bowlful of the milky liquid, they dipped thorns in it and placed them, points upward, on a wooden plank to dry in the sun. The boy told us the lethal thorns would later be scattered in mountain pathways believed to be used by the Lodonites.

"But surely Lodonites don't fight barefoot," I smiled.

"Not intentionally, mirhiliptha," the little boy said. "But even Lodonites lose a sandal once in a while."

Suddenly the little girl's head jerked up. "Funeral pyre."

"Where?" Justin.

She turned around and pointed toward the nearest mountain, where I could make out a tiny flickering light in one of the passes. Justin looked as surprised as I felt. "How did you know?"

"I smelled it," the girl explained.

"I don't smell anything," I said.

Not particularly concerned, the child returned to her work. A full two minutes lapsed before the faint, sweetish odor of burning flesh reached my nostrils. The girl had been right.

I looked around for Adam. He was talking to Commander Fluth, whom I'd not seen approach. Sondra and Ben, accompanied by the one-eyed guard, were going into one of the buildings—a barracks, I supposed. The other guard was watching Justin and me. Alison, as usual, had wandered away.

"They must not know about the epidemic in Lodon," Justin said to me, low. "Otherwise they'd forget all about setting traps and charge over the mountains and win their bloody war."

"Do you think so?" I said. "Would you invade a plague state? I think I'd want to stay as far away as possible."

Justin shrugged. "How much do they know about disease? We didn't recognize it as disease ourselves, at first. I wish there were some way of finding out how much the Kamarians know without giving away how vulnerable the Lodonites are right now."

Our guard was watching us through all this, fully aware that we were speaking low so he could not hear but making no effort to stop us. Adam gestured to us to join him and the Commander.

"Commander Fluth has invited us to join him for a meal." Aha, Adam had made some headway. "I've explained we may not be able to eat what he eats but we have the means of testing it. Where's Ben?"

"In that building," I pointed. "Thank you, Commander, we would like to eat with you." Adam went after Sondra and Ben.

"One of your party is missing," noted Commander Fluth.

"Alison Whitfield," I said.

"Where is she?"

I gave the universal gesture that means "beats me." Fluth nodded to the guard, who went off in search of Alison. When we went to enter the Commander's headquarters building, all our bibblings suddenly took flight. Fluth noticed our surprise and explained, "They never come inside. They go crazy inside a building—just don't like being confined."

By the time the guard brought Alison back, Ben had announced that for this meal at least we were all vegetarians. Ben tried to explain to the Commander that we didn't have the proper juices for digesting the particular meat being served, but Fluth just stared at him blankly, trying to decide whether he was being insulted or not.

"One of those infuriating whims of nature," Adam said lightly. "Kamarians are born stronger than we are, and all we can do about it is complain a lot. We just don't have your body, Commander."

Fluth looked vaguely pleased and told us to sit down. So the man could be flattered. The meat on the table looked downright rancid, and I for one was glad of an excuse not to eat it.

There were two other officers eating with us, both men, and a woman I took to be Fluth's mate. We were served by a young man who looked slightly harassed at having to take care of six extra people. When the last bowl was placed on the table, the woman said, "Thank you, mirhilaves."

Mirhilaves again: the "young man" was a neuter. I could see we were going to have even more trouble identifying neuters in Kamaria than in Lodon—since there was no madness here to isolate the sane neuters for us. Also, in Lodon we'd had the absence of facial hair as a partial guide; here, most of the men were clean-shaven.

Adam made some attempt at talking to Fluth about joining the Federation, but the man really wasn't interested. If we could have offered him something concrete, such as troops to help fight the Lodonites, then he would have listened. But we'd agreed among ourselves not to tell the Kamarians about the alphidium deposits in the mountains, not just yet at any rate. So long as Lodon was such a big question mark, we had to feel our way carefully.

So Adam abandoned his Federation pitch and got Fluth to talk about himself. The Commander turned out to be a bit of a storyteller. He directed most of his talk to Adam, whom he clearly liked; the rest of us he included only when he remembered us. The other two officers joined in, and we were regaled with one anecdote after another designed to illustrate the low cunning and the underhandedness of the Lodonites. I suspected if they ever learned we'd visited Lodon first, our reception would have been considerably less hospitable. All during the meal the four Kamarians kept shooting puzzled glances at Justin. At one point I thought he was going to say something, but he managed to hold his tongue.

The Kamarians showed a pointed lack of curiosity about us and the worlds we came from. At one point Commander Fluth did inquire if our shuttle was for sale, but other than that there was no particular notice paid to our being offworlders. The Kamarians' full attention was on the immediate, the here-and-now. What people in other parts of the galaxy did and thought had no effect on their lives and therefore was of no interest.

"At the end of the last time of weakness," Commander Fluth was saying, "we went up to check the traps." Time of weakness? Winter? "We were working our way across Dead Ridge—slippery there, not many footholds. We were about halfway across when we heard a baby crying. When we'd crossed the ridge, I sent two of my people to find the baby. Well, they found it all right. One of them picked it up and saw too late it had a rope concealed around its waist. The rope pulled loose a wedge that released about a dozen good-sized boulders that had been stacked a little higher up the incline. Six of my people were killed. Does that tell you what kind of animals the Lodonites are? They bait a trap with one of their own babies."

We all stopped eating.

Sondra: "What happened to the baby?"

"Killed too, of course. It was only a neuter, but still it was one of their own."

Meaning sacrificing a neuter infant wasn't quite as bad as killing a male or a female baby?

I was glad when the meal finally ended. We'd accomplished a lot for a first visit; the Kamarians were talking more or less freely with us and might be willing to answer some important questions in subsequent meetings. But it was with relief that I told Commander Fluth we'd be back tomorrow and goodbye for now.

In the shuttle I heard Ben ask Alison where she'd wandered off to this time.

"Here and there. I talked several of the Kamarians into giving me a blood sample. If they have Substance X in their blood too, then we're on the wrong track."

Alison headed straight for the lab the minute we were back aboard the JX-31. The rest of us were still thinking about the baby-baited trap.

Adam: "The real horror of that story is that the Lodonites were appealing to the Kamarians' humanity to lure them to their deaths. Maybe anything goes in a hit-and-run war like this one, but using your enemy's sense of decency as a way of doing him in—well, that's beneath contempt. Inexcusable."

Ben: "Then you believe it?"

"I think so. Did you notice the other three Kamarians at the table? They were nodding and looking disgusted all the time Fluth was telling the story."

Alison came out of the lab with the news that the Kamarians' blood was free of Substance X.

"What do you think?" I asked Adam. "Have the demands of protocol been satisfied? These are very blunt, straightforward people. Do you think we can get on with it?"

"Yes," he said. "Tomorrow we'll ask Fluth why the Kamarians and the Lodonites are fighting a war."

9

"The bibblings cause the war," said Commander Fluth.

I was appalled. Of all the ridiculous things we'd bumped into since we came to this ridiculous planet, this was the most patently absurd. I made a belated attempt to hide my disbelief. "How do they cause the war, Commander?"

"They spend more time with the Lodonites than they do with us," he said.

I examined his face closely. The man was dead serious.

Commander Fluth waited patiently as I formulated my next question. Neither the Kamarians nor the Lodonites could be considered an advanced culture by any scale of measurement, so almost anything was possible.

I took a wild guess. "Are the bibblings magic?"

A look of annoyance crossed the Commander's face. "Forgive me, mirhiliptha, but that is foolish."

So much for local superstition.

"But the bibblings are important enough to cause a war," I persisted.

"Yes, mirhiliptha. They are our strength when they are here. They are our weakness when they desert us for the Lodonites."

I looked over to where Adam was sitting expressionlessly on a bench in Commander Fluth's headquarters. Since Adam was the one the Commander seemed easiest with, we'd agreed that he should talk to Fluth alone first.

They'd been in the headquarters building only ten minutes when Adam sent for me.

"You've tried caging the bibblings, I suppose," I said to Commander Fluth. "To prevent their migrating."

"Not for many years. Bibblings die in confinement."

"You say they are your strength when they're here. You don't literally mean *physical* strength, do you?"

"That is just what I mean. When the bibblings leave, our strength wanes." He paused. "I have told all this to the mirhilancthon."

Adam: "I apologize, Commander, for asking you to explain about the bibblings twice. I feared there may have been some part I failed to understand."

Fluth grunted, nodded his head.

"How," I asked, "can the presence or absence of one particular species of bird control your physical strength?"

"I do not know," the Commander said dispiritedly. "But it has always been so. One third of each year we are strong warriors. Then the bibblings leave and we become weaklings, sapped of all our power. Without the bibblings, Kamaria becomes vulnerable."

I looked helplessly at the man. He obviously thought he'd given me an explanation: a tame bird controlled the Kamarians' physical strength and that's why they were fighting the Lodonites. Sure.

"Do you mean the war is a . . . a holding action?" I floundered. "You're afraid the Lodonites will attack Kamaria while you are, uh, not strong?"

"We *know* they will attack!" he snarled. "Every time of weakness, every time we are helpless to defend ourselves, the Lodonites plant more death in the mountains! Every time! They keep pushing closer and closer! We spend our entire time of strength just pushing them back!" Commander Fluth paused a moment to calm down. "Now I can talk no longer. The bibblings will be leaving us soon. We have time for only one more campaign, and I must see to my troops."

We murmured the expected courtesies and left.

Outside, we told the others what Fluth had said about the bibblings and sympathized with their expressions of dismay. We couldn't very well send a report to Culloden saying the war was being fought over a bunch of birds. We'd asked the question we'd been sent here to ask, but we were no nearer a solution than when we'd first landed. The Lodonites and the Kamarians had been systematically slaughtering each other for generations, and the only thing resembling a reason we'd uncovered was this cockamamie story about the bibblings.

Sondra: "But what then? Didn't you try to pin him down?"

"I was trying to, but he dismissed us," I said. "He was busy—getting ready for his last campaign before the bibblings leave."

"Campaign?" Justin perked up. "Is Fluth going to lead a campaign himself?"

"That's what it sounded like."

"Damn, I'd love to see that! Do you suppose he'd let an observer tag along?"

"We can ask," said Adam. "Come on."

The two men went into the headquarters building and came back out a few minutes later, Justin looking pleased. "He's still not comfortable around me, but he said okay. I wonder what it is about me that bothers him so."

"Maybe you'll get a chance to ask him on the campaign," Sondra said dryly. "You know, comrades-in-arms sitting around the old campfire, showing your wounds, swapping lies . . ."

Justin laughed. "You're making a joke of it, but it may work out just that way. I'm certainly going to give it my best shot."

Adam, Sondra, and I spent the next week in the army camp and a few of the villages, looking at everything, asking questions. A vote of Kamarian confidence: after the second day, our guards had failed to appear. Ben and Alison were holed up in the ship's lab, still trying to break down Substance X. Justin was in the mountains with Commander Fluth.

The soldiers talked to us openly, working hurriedly as they did. A near-feverish quality in their movements: they were trying to get as many traps set up in the mountains as possible before the bibblings left. No question in their minds but that they would become weak and helpless once the birds migrated.

Shuttle-hopping from one village to the next: the further we got from the mountains, the less military activity we found. The bibblings' deadline was drawing near, we were told; military supplies could no longer be transported to the mountains in time. The villagers were directing all their efforts toward digging in against "the time of weakness." Children were everywhere, but only the very youngest seemed to have time for play. Everyone else had a job to do.

"How tired the women look," Adam remarked. "The men seem to be holding up better."

Sondra grunted. "Try having a baby every year and see how perky-fresh you feel. And the women here go to war as well—the two activities don't seem to be mutually exclusive."

"Message received," Adam smiled. "And the last I heard, child care still takes a little time and effort too. Wonder where all the Lodonite children were?" He watched four of the younger Kamarian children playing a complicated game involving a ball and two sticks. "The Kamarians, at least, are assured of a future—sturdy-looking youngsters, aren't they?"

"And look at the adulthood waiting for them," Sondra, glumly. "Perpetual warfare. This is one reason I have so little sympathy with underdeveloped worlds. Invariably they *manufacture* children—the same way we'd manufacture a tool to do a specific job. On most frontier-type worlds it's done to provide the family with unpaid workers—a man fathers as many children as he can to get help working the land or whatever. Here, they make little soldiers. And the children's mothers all work fantastic con jobs on themselves—they *have* to believe laying eggs is the highest human achievement possible or else they'd go mad."

"I think I'd go mad here anyway," I said. "Could you live in a constant state of warfare? I couldn't."

"Yes you could. These people have managed to make their war tolerable by restricting all the actual fighting to the no-man's-land in the mountains. Neither side has been invaded. If your country's occupied by an enemy, that's one thing. But as long as the fighting's kept away from home, you can live with it."

It was Sondra who pointed out the significance of every village's having at least one still in operation. Nobody was drinking the alcohol. It was all being stored in earthenware jugs, many of which were sent to the army camp. Adam and Sondra and I couldn't remember having seen a single Kamarian soldier take a drink in all the time we'd been here; and there was no *trang* on the table during the one meal we'd shared with the Kamarians. The alcohol was being laid in for the future—just one more supply that was going to be needed.

Sondra: "What this means is that the Kamarians are so firmly convinced they won't be able to fight after the bibblings leave that they don't even bother to try. For all practical purposes, the birds *do* rob the Kamarians of their strength when they migrate. Now the Lodonites have a real reason for drinking—but the Kamarians *think* they do, so their reason becomes just as real. Don't underestimate the power of suggestion—we mustn't think of their bibbling-belief as just superstition."

In one village we watched an elderly neuter putting stoppers into the jugs. Every once in a while the neuter would dump the contents of one of the jugs into a small vat. Adam asked why.

"Wrong smell," the neuter said.

Adam sniffed a jug doomed for the vat. "Smells just like the others to me."

"Try it."

Adam tipped up the jug and tasted the *trang*. On the instant his face dissolved into a picture of misery, and he spat the stuff on the ground. The old neuter cackled and emptied the jug into the vat.

We meandered away from the still and came to a river at the edge of the village. The water was so clear the weeds growing among the rocks at the bottom were visible. We sat on the bank and watched a tree branch carrying two bibblings float by. The branch hit a snag; the two golden birds lifted gracefully into the air, their outstretched wings barely moving in the breeze. The river current worked the branch loose from the snag; the bibblings glided back to their perch and resumed their downstream boat ride.

Another bibbling had settled itself on Adam's knee. I rested my hand on the golden feathers and felt the small body vibrating under my touch. A purring bird?

Sondra was looking abstracted. "Something peculiar going on here."

Adam: "What?"

"That neuter who gave you the bad *trang* to taste. *Smelling* the difference between good and bad alcohol. I talked to some farmers in the last village—at the time I wasn't sure I understood, but it seemed to me they were talking about *smelling* whether the grain was ready to harvest or not. And I'm sure one of them said something about detecting the odor of illness in some herd animals he was raising. *Smelling* illness? Can that be possible?"

An odd look came over Adam's face. "That would explain . . . A couple of days ago in the army camp, I thought it might be enlightening to talk to some soldiers who'd just come back from the mountains. I asked a woman which was their barracks. She took me to one of the buildings but then told me they weren't there. The door was closed, so I asked her how she knew they weren't there. She said she'd be able to smell them if they were inside. I thought she was having a little fun at my expense, but now . . ."

I told them about the child who could smell the funeral pyre long before I could.

Sondra: "When one of the senses is developed beyond any 'normal' range, it's usually in compensation for the failure of another of the senses. But the Kamarians have the normal use of *all* their senses—plus this exceptional sense of smell. I wonder why."

We all wondered why. "Do you suppose the Lodonites have the same extra sense of smell?" I asked. "They must—since they're the same race as the Kamarians. Remember that awful stench in the Lodonite army camp? It bothered us, but it must have been sheer torture to them."

Adam: "Maybe that's the real reason they'd drunk themselves insensible. To kill the smell."

Justin was back. He was tired and dirty, but his eyes glistened with excitement.

"This campaign was no trap-setting expedition," he said. "It was real honest-to-God old-time guerrilla warfare. The kind I've never seen except in historical tapes. Fluth is one hell of a commander! Damn, it was an eyeopener. I've never really understood that die-for-glory bit, but it makes a little more sense now. Fluth's soldiers were magnificent—truly courageous people."

We were sitting in the wardroom of the JX-31 listening to Justin tell his war stories, one bloody skirmish after another. But it was something that Justin tossed in as a sort of minor curiosity that made us sit up and pay attention. Justin told us that Commander Fluth had detected an ambush by smelling the food the Lodonites carried with them.

"One more piece of evidence," said Alison, who'd taken a special interest in our stories about the Kamarians' extraordinary olfactory abilities. "Sondra's right—there shouldn't be such a highly developed sense of smell without the failure of another of the senses. But there it is." She explained to Justin what we'd learned.

"Did you get to talk to Commander Fluth?" I asked him. "About why you make him so nervous?"

"Yes, but I didn't really learn anything. Fluth himself brought the subject up, one night after I—" He broke off abruptly and shot a glance around the wardroom. "Fluth apologized to me," Justin went on hurriedly, "for mistaking me for a neuter. He said he'd never made that mistake before in his life—in fact, he didn't even *know* anyone who'd ever made such a mistake. He was really quite earnest about it, as if it were important I understand. I told him as long as my wife and I both knew I was male, being called 'mirhilaves' wasn't going to hurt me."

"Then what?"

"Then *I* made a mistake. I asked him if neuters were considered inferior in Kamaria—and he closed down on me. It was a tactless question or else tactlessly put, but Fluth shut down completely. He announced stiffly that all Kamaria was grateful to its neuters, that without the neuters the war would have been lost long ago. And that was his final word. The subject was closed."

"All right," I said, "so let's open another one. Now tell us what you started to tell us before you changed your mind." He grinned sheepishly. "Come on, Justin. Give."

Big sigh. "I didn't just observe. I helped. Oh, I didn't do any fighting. But I bound wounds, carried supplies, helped repair equipment. The night Fluth apologized to me was at a time they were all feeling grateful to me—I'd shown them how to move faster over an exposed rockface by using a climbing net. An old trick—goes back at least to Alexander the Great." Justin took a breath and looked me straight in the eye. "I know a diplomatic mission is supposed to be impartial, but I think you ought to know I no longer find it possible to be impartial. I want the Kamarians to win this one."

We all laughed.

Justin, puzzled. "What did I say funny?"

"No diplomatic mission is ever truly impartial," I told him. "That's an unrealizable ideal, Justin, and it's best just to accept it and proceed accordingly. Culloden is quite willing to settle for the *appearance* of impartiality from his agents. What goes on underneath the appearance is our business."

"I tried to tell you that before we left," Sondra smiled.

Justin grunted. "Guess I should have listened."

Now that we were all together again, I brought up something that had been bothering me the last day or two. "I'd like you all to think back to the time we spent in Lodon. About how many neuters would you say we saw there?"

"There are plenty of them in the mountains," said Justin.

"Not in the mountains. In the army camp and the village."

Ben: "There was Garrinel. And the other neuters carrying water and food. Five or six of them altogether."

Sondra: "The firefighters in the village. Half a dozen?"

"And didn't we pass one on the road to the village?" said Alison. "That makes a dozen, maybe fifteen. Most of the Lodonites we saw were men or women."

I turned to Justin. "Did you see any male or female Lodonite soldiers in the mountains?"

"No, we didn't. I thought it was odd, running into one squad of neuters after another. Do you think the neuters are doing *all* the fighting for the Lodonites after all?"

"Looks like it. Now, roughly, how many neuters are in the Kamarian army camp?"

Sondra said, "That's a little harder. Neuters aren't so easy to spot here. The only one I can be sure of is the one who served us when we ate with Commander Fluth. And only then because he—*it*—was addressed as 'mirhilaves.' "

"What are you getting at, Val?" Adam.

"Just this. I asked one of the Kamarian soldiers where the neuters were. He said in the villages, on the farms, preparing food and clothing for their 'time of weakness.' The time after the bibblings leave."

Justin whistled. "Just the opposite of the Lodonites. *Their* neuters fight in the mountains while the others stay below. In Kamaria it's the men and women who do the fighting. These two races are opposite in every way."

"But they're not two races," Sondra objected. "They're not even two branches of the same race, they *are* the same race. Same language, same degree of social development, same everything."

"But still opposite," insisted Justin.

"But still opposite," Sondra yielded, exasperated.

"And remember," said Ben, "the Kamarians have no Substance X in their bloodstream. That's the important opposite."

10

Commander Fluth was trying to persuade me to leave the planet.

"Life is not pleasant after the bibblings go," he said to me. "Return home, mirhiliptha. Take your companions and leave. You will be safe, and there is nothing you can do to help us here."

I was beginning to think he was right. Everyone in the Kamarian army was working at fever pitch: no more time for answering questions, no more time for satisfying the curiosity of meddling offworlders. No time left.

"Commander Fluth, why have the Kamarians not won this war? We've flown over Lodon"—well, we had—"and you seem to have all the advantages. Even the terrain works in your favor."

"Ah, but the Lodonites have the bibblings two-thirds of the year. During our time of weakness they make great advances in the mountains. It takes all our time of strength just to undo what they have done."

"Have you ever tried negotiating for peace?"

"That was last done in my father's time. Both Lodon and Kamaria agreed to stop fighting. But when the bibblings returned to us, we found the Lodonites had used their time of strength to build new traps and weapons. We were forced to do the same."

"Would you be interested in trying again? With a little outside help? The Federation is more than willing to provide assistance if you want it—advisers, arbitrators, errand-runners, anything you want."

"The only thing that will help is the defeat of Lodon. There is no other way."

"Surely that isn't the only solution, Commander."

"Tell me a better one. Yes, we could negotiate with the Lodonites again. And yes, those underhanded liars would probably agree to a truce—if they saw some advantage in it. And the minute we laid down our arms they would be swarming all over the mountains, intent on destroying us. You must understand, mirhiliptha, Lodonites are vultures. They prey on the helpless. They are not people you can talk to. They're not to be trusted. Ever."

"But if they knew the Federation was policing the mountains, making sure both sides kept to their agreement—"

"It would still make no difference. Mirhiliptha, you don't understand. You simply cannot reason with Lodonites."

Did he know what was going on in Lodon after all? The condition the Lodonites were in now, they certainly couldn't be reasoned with. Perhaps we'd been too quick to assume the Lodonite madness was only a recent development.

"Commander, when did this war begin?"

He waved an arm helplessly. "So many generations ago, no one remembers."

That long. And the Lodonite disease had persisted for countless generations without extinguishing the race? I couldn't believe it.

"How did it all start? There must have been a specific incident, or a series of incidents. What happened?"

Commander Fluth shrugged. "It has always been so."

I shook my head. "Commander, that—" I'd started to say that didn't make any sense but caught myself in time. "That's something I'm afraid I don't understand. Everything has a beginning. Did the Kamarians just wake up one morning to find the Lodonites had occupied the mountains? Was there any kind of formal declaration of war? What do the Lodonites *want*?"

He looked at me as if I weren't quite bright. "They want the bibblings."

Then GIVE them the bibblings, for crying out loud!
"Commander, when the bibblings migrate, where do they go? They go to Lodon, don't they?"

"Yes. And stay there two-thirds of each year."

"Then what's the problem? The Lodonites have the bibblings part of the year, you have them part of the year. Is that worth killing over?"

I watched the Commander gear himself up to make one more attempt. "Mirhiliptha, without the bibblings, Kamaria will die. Without the bibblings to end our time of weakness, we'd die out in a generation, maybe two. The Lodonites want the bibblings all year round. But we *need* them. Bibblings are life, mirhiliptha."

It sounded too simple. "You told me the bibblings can't be caged, that they die in captivity. If you can't cage them, neither can the Lodonites. I'm sorry to be so dense, Commander, but I just don't see how winning a war would affect the migration of birds."

He shook his head tiredly. "The bibblings will cross the mountains when they want to, whatever we do. But without an enemy on the other side of the mountains, we could follow the bibblings when they leave. Since they won't stay with us, then we could go with them."

"Into Lodon?"

"Yes. And back again to Kamaria when the time comes."

"And the Lodonites want the same thing? To cross into Kamaria when the bibblings leave Lodon?"

Commander Fluth's mouth was a straight line; a vein throbbed at his temple. "Twice as long!" he burst out. "They have the bibblings twice as long as we do! And that's not enough for them. No, they want to cut us out completely—to, to keep the bibblings all to themselves!"

I thought: *And isn't that exactly what you want?*

The Commander was dejected after his outburst. "Do you see, mirhiliptha? We *have* to fight the Lodonites. We have no choice. Do you understand?"

I was afraid I did. It looked as if the Lodonites and the Kamarians both were using the bibblings as an excuse for what was nothing more than a plain old-fashioned land-grab.

I left the Commander and went looking for Adam. I found him strolling through the camp, a bibbling on each shoulder, unsuccessfully looking for someone who wasn't too busy to talk to him. I told him what I'd learned.

"Well, well, well," he mused. " 'Twould appear our noble Kamarians aren't quite so noble after all. Utterly fascinating, the elaborate rationalizations people work out to justify doing what they want to do. Especially when they know what they want to do isn't very nice. The Culloden said no territorial issue was involved, but our Grand Pooh-Bah seems to have been in error this time. Of course, all he had to go on were those early scouting reports. That's the trouble with preliminary studies, they're always so *preliminary*. Now we have something to work with, at least."

"But we still have only Fluth's word for it," I said doubtfully. "I'd like to hear the Lodonites' side of it. Do you think we should go back to Lodon? Talk to the neuters, ask them about the bibblings?"

"Yes, alas," Adam sighed. He no more wanted to go back to that madhouse than I did. "We ought to confirm that the Lodonites blame the war on the birds the same as the Kamarians do. Though to tell you the truth, I'm having trouble conceiving of that pitiful nation on the other side of the mountains fostering territorial ambitions at all. Two-thirds of the population can't even feed themselves—how can they think of conquering Kamaria? Suddenly it's become very important to know how long that epidemic has been raging in Lodon."

"How long the Lodonites have been incapacitated, you mean? Yes, that would make a difference. Perhaps—"

I was going to suggest that we try talking to Commander Zizzi again, but the two bibblings on Adam's shoulders suddenly took off with an abruptness that startled us both.

The air was instantly filled with the sound of hundreds and hundreds of fluttering wings. As if in response to a silent signal, every bibbling in camp had taken flight.

Streaks of gold flashed by, climbing high, higher, until they filled the sky. The migration had begun.

A Byzantine sky! A breathtakingly beautiful Byzantine sky, with the gold leaf flaking off to reveal an underlay of blue. A flickering golden ceiling that moved over our heads as we watched. Physical reaction: I became dizzy, disoriented, had to look down at my feet on the solid ground.

Sondra and Justin came running up to us, Sondra's eyes sparkling, excited. "Did you ever see anything like this before?"

I never did. I'd only seen birds migrating in flocks, a few at a time. Somebody would point and say *look* and you'd look and that'd be the end of it. But wave after wave of golden birds passed over our heads, with no end in sight—stunning, elusive, magical.

"Look at the Kamarians," said Justin.

A shock: every Kamarian face a tragic mask. Tears streaming down cheeks, a woman throwing up, one young man shaking his fist at the golden sky. Sondra went over to the woman who was ill, but the woman just gestured her away.

"Will someone please explain to me," said Adam, "how I'm supposed to raise the shuttle up through *that*?"

I hadn't thought of that. It wasn't unknown for a large aircraft to be brought down by little bird-bodies blocking the vents.

"This can't last long," Sondra. "Can it? How many bibblings can there be in this country?"

More than we'd dreamed possible, as it turned out. We waited. The daylight was beginning to go and there was still no let-up in the number of birds blanketing the sky, separating us from the JX-31. We always tried to be back on the ship by nightfall. With no moons to reflect light, Kamaria was pitch-black after sunset.

Adam: "Let's give it a try. I'll take us up slowly—if the birds don't feel inclined to part and let us through, then we'll just come back and wait it out."

But either the shuttle scared them or else the bibblings were in a cooperative mood, for they separated immediately at our approach and let us pass. On the ship we dragged Alison and Ben out of the lab and told them to look through the scanners.

Ben: "What is it? I can't make it out. Looks like a cloth of gold laid over the continent."

"A *moving* cloth of gold," Alison amended. "Ah— nothing but green islands now." Our orbit was taking us to the other side of the planet. "Was it the bibblings?"

Sondra: "Got it in one."

The next morning the migration was still going on, so all six of us went down in the shuttle. Again the bibblings left a big hole for us to pass through and Adam touched us down as near to Commander Fluth's headquarters as he could manage.

The Kamarians wouldn't talk to us; they weren't even talking to one another. Fluth stood with his hands on his hips, staring glumly into the distance where the birds were streaming into the mountain passes. The young man who'd shaken his fist at the sky the day before was still there, had been there all night from the looks of him. I watched that beautiful Byzantine sky until I got a crick in my neck.

The birds flew all that day and until a little after noon on the next day. Two full days, and they were gone. All of them. I could feel it in my bones: not a single bibbling remained in Kamaria.

An anomaly: an army camp without noise. More: without any sound whatsoever. Even the animals seemed intimidated by the birds' migration and stood motionless, quiet. I have never before or since listened to a silence like the one in Kamaria at that moment. Even Adam and I didn't know what to say to each other. We were beginning to understand the despair that overtook the Kamarians when their bibblings left them. The Kamarians had lost something precious to them.

Eventually signs of life began to return. Some of the Kamarians continued working desultorily at the tasks in which they'd been engaged when the bibblings first took flight. Some were weeping; some sat as if hypnotized. Others walked away from their work without a backward glance and began trudging zombielike down the various roads that led to the villages. Commander Fluth returned to his headquarters building and closed the door.

We stayed on in the camp for several days and found ourselves watching what amounted to a transfer of responsibility. Male and female soldiers who'd been in the mountains when the birds migrated were coming back— hordes of them, many more than we'd realized. Every one of them walked heavily, with more than just fatigue weighing on them. Their pinched, closed faces, their dragging feet, their very posture all proclaimed defeat. And their eyes! I'd seen those haunted eyes once before, in Goya's picture of human degradation called *The Witches' Sabbath*. If we hadn't known about the bibblings, we'd have concluded that the Kamarians had just lost the war.

Most of the returning soldiers plodded through the camp without stopping, shrugging off weapons and equipment as they passed. They looked neither right nor left, intent only on getting home. A few stayed in the camp, collecting the gear dropped by the homeward-bound soldiers. These few performed their tasks halfheartedly, as if it didn't really matter what they did.

At the end of the second day the neuters started coming—singly, in pairs, then by the dozens. They came from the villages, the farms, wherever they had been during the time of strength. They armed themselves with the equipment left by the returning men and women, and without anyone giving them orders marched off to take their places in the mountains. Commander Fluth's door remained closed.

"So that's it," said Adam. "The males and females do the fighting during the time of strength, but it's up to the neuters to hold the line during the time of weakness. Just like the Lodonites."

We all looked at one another uneasily. If it was indeed "just like the Lodonites," that meant that before long our sane Kamarians would metamorphose into raving madmen.

11

We didn't have long to wait.

First sign: one of the male soldiers still in camp gave a great howl of rage and tried to strangle his female companion. She slipped away from him; and while the other soldiers looked on listlessly, she began a deadly game of hide-and-seek.

An effective ploy. The maddened male seemed unable to concentrate on one objective long and was distracted by almost anything that caught his eye. One pebble out of hundreds on the ground held him a full minute. Then: furiously pounding a barrel with both fists, trying to break through wood and iron with flesh and bone, systematically turning his hands into ground meat. The woman he'd attacked eased up behind him and placed an earthenware jug on the ground nearby. Then she ran as hard as she could toward one of the village roads, and we never saw her again.

The soldier eventually noticed the jug. He broke off his assault on the barrel and fumbled with the stopper. When he couldn't get it out with his bloody hands, he wrapped both arms around the jug and worried the stopper loose with his teeth. He drank long and deeply, as if his life depended on it. After a while he was snoring on the ground, harmless as a baby. The other soldiers who had been watching all this eyed one another sadly, and moved farther apart.

"Just like the Londonites," repeated Adam. "They've

found that drunkenness renders them harmless. So they lay in a store of *trang* against the time they go berserk."

We were all wearing filter masks, at Alison's insistence. If the "time of weakness" was indeed the disease we'd seen in Lodon, then we needed to protect ourselves against the possibility that Substance X might be airborne.

"But they can't stay drunk all the time," Sondra objected. "They'd all die of cirrhosis of the liver, if nothing else."

"Probably this violent condition appears only in sporadic seizures," said Alison. "Not all the Lodonites were violent, remember. I'd say this disease waxes and wanes. As a depressant, alcohol makes an effective temporary antidote. *Mansola*—safely asleep. When that man sobers up, he might not be violent at all—for a while. Let's wait and see." She edged over to the sleeping soldier and touched a microscope slide to his bloody hands.

"Looking for Substance X?" I asked Ben. He nodded.

But waiting and seeing was becoming risky: there were other outbursts of violence, starting up here and there without warning, forcing us to huddle in semi-concealment at the side of the headquarters building. A wagon was set on fire. We watched in horror as several soldiers hurled themselves headfirst against Commander Fluth's closed door. A woman sat trying to bite through a bundle of firewood. Two young men were eating grass. Late-arriving neuters detoured around the frenzied men and women, once in a while stopping to place a jug near the more dangerous ones before proceeding on their march to the mountains.

Ben: "Where's Alison?"

We all went to look for her; no one cared to venture out through the camp alone. For the first time in all the years I'd known her, I felt irritation at Alison's habit of wandering away whenever the notion took her. She should have seen the camp was becoming dangerous.

Fortunately she hadn't gone far; we found her talking to two neuters. They were staring suspiciously at this strange filter-masked offworlder who seemed to want nothing more out of life than a sample of their blood. But finally one of them held out a hand and allowed a finger to be pricked, and the other neuter followed suit. Alison was still thanking them when they shrugged and resumed their journey to the mountains.

Suddenly Commander Fluth's door flew open. The Commander himself lurched through the doorway, his arms and legs twitching and jerking, his mouth drooling white foam.

"A dancer," Ben said. "Let's get him."

It took all five of us to hold the Commander still while Alison took her blood sample. Not the Commander Fluth I knew: I was holding down the arm of an utter stranger. I saw the terrified and terrifying face of Blake's mad Nebuchadnezzar and had to look away. When we released him Fluth danced away, not even knowing we were there.

"Now back to the ship," I said.

"No!" protested Alison. "We have to be here when that soldier sobers up. How else will we know whether the violence is steady or erratic?"

"No, Alison," I said firmly. "It's getting too dangerous to stay here. What if some of the Kamarians get it into their heads to smash up our shuttle while we're waiting? We've got to get back to the ship while we still can."

She yielded with good grace. We dodged our way back to the shuttle, playing the same deadly game of hide-and-seek that the fleeing woman had played earlier. Once Ben tripped and fell, his big body barely missing a Kamarian woman who lay curled on the ground, hugging a jug. But we reached the shuttle without further mishap, and Adam lifted us off and got us back inside the JX-31.

We tossed our filter masks into the disposal. The Barks and Adam and I sat silently in the wardroom while the Whitfields analyzed their blood samples. There was a mystery here, and each one of us was trying to puzzle it out on his own. Obviously I'd been wrong: this was no simple land-grab we were dealing with. The "time of weakness" was the time when madness swept the land, when men and women became too irrational even to think of invading a neighboring country. Fluth and the other

Kamarians wanted to follow the bibblings into Lodon for one very simple reason: to retain their sanity.

Alison and Ben came out of the lab. Commander Fluth's and the drunken soldier's blood showed the presence of Substance X. The neuters' blood was clean.

"It just doesn't make sense," Sondra said in a tired voice. "Fluth must have been right—it seems clear the bibblings are responsible for this. But how? How can the presence of the birds in Lodon cause an epidemic in Kamaria? And vice versa? I can understand a bird's carrying a parasite that *causes* disease—but this is just the reverse! How can the birds *prevent* this madness?"

Adam: "Is it possible that the bibblings carry some sort of neutralizing organism? Something that defuses Substance X?"

"It's possible," Ben nodded. "Perhaps the disease is hereditary after all. I'm beginning to think the presence of Substance X in the bloodstream is a normal biological condition for these people, something all the males and females are born with. Only the neuters have a 'pure' bloodstream—free from Substance X."

"That's why the Kamarians had twice as many troops in the mountains as the Lodonites," said Justin. "When we first got here, I mean. Two-thirds of the Kamarian population—the males and the females—were engaged in combat, directly or indirectly. But only a third of the Lodonites—the neuters—were sane enough to fight."

"What about transfusions?" I asked. "Put some of that healthy neuter blood into the males and females."

"Wouldn't do any good," said Ben. "The neuters' blood contains no special complement system to fight the effects of Substance X, because there's no Substance X in their blood to fight. Whatever cleans Substance X out of the blood—during the time of strength—it doesn't come from their own bodies. It comes from outside."

"So we're back to the bibblings," said Adam.

"We're back to the bibblings."

"In short," snapped Sondra, "you don't know anything at all about it." She spoke so sharply we all looked at her in surprise.

"We're doing our best, Sondra," Ben said mildly.

"Then your best isn't very good, is it, Dr. Whitfield? All you're doing is guessing."

Adam stepped in quickly. "That's all any of us can do right now. I think we'd better get some sleep before we try making any decisions—we're all on edge. Alison, how about breaking out the tranquilizers?"

Sondra jumped up and faced Adam. "Earthman speak with oiled tongue!" she shrieked—and lunged at him.

Her attack was so unexpected that it took us a moment to understand what was happening. Belatedly we rushed toward them. Sondra had Adam down on the floor, biting at his neck and ears, beating at his head with her fists, growling and panting like an animal. It was ugly, and frightening. I grabbed Sondra around the waist but couldn't budge her. Adam should have hit her, hard—but he was taken by surprise even more than the rest of us. By the time we finally pulled her back, Sondra had chewed away half of Adam's right ear.

I held his bleeding head in my lap while Alison ran for the antiseptic. Ben and Justin managed to strap the now-raving Sondra into a seat.

"A sedative!" shouted Justin. "For God's sake, Whitfield, give her a sedative!"

"Too risky," panted Ben. "If she's infected with Substance X, there's no telling how she'd react."

"Use the local antidote," I said. "Get her drunk."

Then I gave my whole attention to Adam. I helped Alison as much as I could, holding his head steady as she cleaned up his ear.

"I'm putting on plastiflesh now, Adam," she said, working quickly. "Which means you'll be running around with half an ear as long as we're here. A new ear flap can be grafted on when we get back—no problem there." She looked up at me. "It's not serious, Val. It looks terrible, but it's not. He'll be all right."

I smiled a weak thank you at her and bent over to kiss Adam's forehead. "Are you feeling dizzy? Can you walk?"

"Sure," he said thickly and struggled to his feet. I

glanced over at Sondra. She was quieter now, coughing sporadically as Justin forced brandy down her throat.

It took us an hour to get everything under control again. Sondra lay strapped in her cabin, sleeping off her drunk. Adam was in our cabin, heavily sedated, resting as comfortably as could be expected. We'd cleaned up the blood, and I had changed my clothes. Then the remaining four of us sat down to decide what to do.

"There's only one thing *to* do," Justin said angrily. "Get the hell away from this damned planet and back to a Federation hospital where she can receive the full treatment. Adam, too," he added as an afterthought.

"Don't think so," said Ben. "The Federation knows nothing about this disease. Its origin is here, and its cause will have to be found here. Besides, our pilot's in no condition to fly us back. What about Adam, Alison?"

"He'll be able to function in a few days," she said. "I'm going to keep him under sedation for the next twenty-four hours or so. And then he'll be woozy-headed for a while. But he'll be all right."

Ben: "Good. You understand, don't you, that this shoots hell out of my theory that the male and female members of this race are born with Substance X already in their bloodstream? Sondra's got it, all right. I checked her blood."

"Which brings us to the main point," I said. "We're obviously just as vulnerable as the Kamarians. Since they were right about the bibblings, that means the Lodonites have probably recovered from their madness and we'd be better off with them. Those filter masks certainly didn't protect Sondra."

"No," sighed Alison. "Either they're not adequate to filter out Substance X or else we put them on too late. Or maybe Substance X isn't airborne after all."

I was so tired I was sick. And I was sick with worry about Adam and Sondra, sick with fear that we wouldn't be able to solve the mystery of the bibblings. I told the others I was going to check on Adam.

I opened the cabin door—and stopped dead. Adam was in the center of the small cabin, his whole body twitching and jerking, elbows and knees pumping, eyes glazed, white flecks in the corners of his mouth. He had dislodged the plastiflesh on his ear, and the bleeding had started up again.

I screamed for help.

We had to settle for just strapping him down so he wouldn't hurt himself. Alison and Ben positively forbade the introduction of alcohol into his already "sedated" system. I sat holding him and trying to calm him until Ben picked me up bodily and carried me out of the cabin. We stood in the corridor, looking at each other, wondering who would be next.

I was next.

I have no memory of that ugly time, except for the sensation of fingers in my mouth, prying my jaws apart. I had one brief glimpse of Justin Bark's anxious face, and I felt brandy burning rivulets down the inside of my throat. Then nothing.

Later—much later—I struggled for an eternity to open my gummed-shut eyes. *Don't panic, don't panic! You're not blind!* Just work those eyes open. Mouth foul, head pounding, stomach in turmoil. Achy bones. At last I got my eyes open and stared up at a shimmering stretch of blue overhead. Disorientation upon awakening in a strange place: I was lying on my back on the open ground underneath a sky that looked close enough to touch.

And a bibbling was perched on my arm.

12

It was Justin who'd saved us. He alone had remained untouched by the virulent Substance X that had reduced the rest of us to idiocy within a matter of hours.

Sondra was bending over me, her face white and drawn. Clutched in each hand: a bibbling. "How do you feel?"

"More dead than alive. Adam?"

"Sleeping. So are Alison and Ben. Justin told me what I did to Adam. Valerie, I . . . I didn't know what I was doing—"

"I know," I said, and reached out my hand toward her. The sudden movement startled the bibbling on my arm; the bird took to the air and was gone. Sondra quickly placed one of her bibblings on my stomach; the bird hooked its claws around my belt and settled down.

"Thank God they're so tame," Sondra said with a nervous laugh.

I wasn't thinking clearly yet. "Bibblings. Then we're . . . ?"

"We're in Lodon. Justin says the Whitfields both came down with the disease while he was still pouring brandy into you. Ben gave him a hard time—he's a strong man, you know. But eventually Justin got us all drunk enough so he could manage. He loaded us into the shuttle and took off for Lodon. He looked for an uninhabited stretch until he found this glade where we are now. He says all he could think of was finding the bibblings, that the bibblings were the only way to cure us."

"Well, obviously he was right." With a trembly hand I stroked the velvety creature on my stomach. "Where's Justin now?"

"Taking a nap. He's exhausted, Val. Playing nursemaid to five lunatics for three days can't have been easy."

Three days. I moved the bibbling to my shoulder and sat up. I waited until the dizziness passed and then got to my feet with Sondra's help. She led me to where Adam was lying.

His face was chalk-white, his breathing shallow. His half an ear looked all right, but he was weak from loss of blood as well as from the disease.

"He needs blood," I told Sondra.

"I'll wake Justin. I'm still too wobbly to try handling the shuttle myself. What's his blood type?"

"A-positive." The shuttle carried an emergency medical kit, but the whole blood was kept on board the JX-31.

Justin came over to look at Adam before he left. His handsome face was drawn with fatigue and there were circles under his eyes. He touched my shoulder. "I'm going to bring back some food and other supplies. What about glucose for Adam?"

Glucose, my God, yes. I should have thought of it. I nodded and Justin left.

Sondra and I waited with Adam, my fingers on his faint and quavery pulse. After a while Adam's lips started moving. Then he opened his mouth wide, as if stretching his jaw, and shut it again. Open, and shut.

Sondra: "That's exactly what you did right before you woke up."

It seemed hours before Justin returned. Justin held the blood- and glucose-dispensers as I fitted the tubes to Adam's arm. Adam came to while we were still feeding him.

I waited until his eyes focused and he recognized me. "Hello, love," I said. "Enjoying your dinner?"

"Let's screw," he whispered weakly.

That's my Adam.

After a while he fell into a deep, natural sleep. His pulse was steadier and a little stronger. "I think he'll be all right," I told the Barks, "but I wish one of the Whitfields could look at him."

Alison and Ben were lying near each other, she curled up in a ball, he flat on his back with his arms straight out at right angles. Ben's big body labored with the difficulties of respiration.

"My God, what happened to her eye?" I exclaimed. Alison's left eye was swollen and discolored, a real shiner.

"Ben did that," said Justin. "He flattened her with one blow—she tried to stop him from smashing one of the consoles. She went down like a rag doll, and stayed unconscious until I finally got Ben drunk. By the time I got to her, her arms and legs were beginning to twitch—I think she would have been a dancer."

"Justin," I said curiously, "what did I do?"

He hesitated. "You tried to set the wardroom on fire."

I sighed. "We certainly managed to hit all the bases, didn't we?"

Alison woke up a few hours later, but Ben didn't come around until early the next morning. We were all mobile to varying degrees by then, even Adam. We were gathered around Ben as he first stretched his jaws and then struggled to open his eyes.

He took one look at Alison's black eye and began to cry.

Instinctively we all reached toward him, wanting to hug him, to reassure him. Then we were all hugging one another, finding comfort in touching. We'd had a narrow escape, and we were still scared.

When the emotionalism of the moment passed, we were first amused by our spontaneous group grope and then serious.

"You've got to be impressed by the Kamarians and the Lodonites," Sondra said. "We've had only a tiny brush with something they live with all their lives. How do they stand it? How can you face life positively when you know that once a year, regular as clockwork, you're going to go stark raving mad?"

Adam: "Wonder what their suicide rate is. But maybe it's true the human mind can adjust to anything."

"Sondra," I said, "do you remember back during our hypnobriefing, you objected to women's being 'honored' simply because they gave birth? As if it were some sort of special achievement? Well, it *is* a special achievement, isn't it? With both war and disease thinning their ranks, these people must look upon every new life as a buffer against the possible extinction of their race. Of course childbearing is honored."

Sondra nodded slowly. "It makes sense now. All this, and they still manage to keep their will to life. I admire them. It'd be understandable if they'd just given up generations ago. But they're still here. I admire them."

We all did, now that we understood a little better what they were up against. Our initial purpose of trying to find a way to bring about a truce between Lodon and Kamaria was sheer folly so long as both nations were subject to seasonal madness. The war was nothing compared to the disease.

Justin: "Do you still think Culloden will make excuses about sending in a pathology team? When he learns five of his own people caught the disease?"

We all thought the question over carefully. "Yes," said five voices.

Justin made a vulgar noise.

Adam: "Money, Justin, money. The pathology team is only the beginning—epidemic control is an expensive operation. Culloden isn't going to stick his neck out and recommend that the Federation pour all that money into a nonmember world—*unless* he has a guarantee that the Federation's investment will bring back a profit. What we've got to do is provide him with that guarantee."

Nobody said "How?" but that's what we were all thinking.

We stayed on in the glade a while, resting and doing mild exercises to build up our strength. Justin made periodic trips back to the ship for supplies. Alison's eye was clearing up, only a sick-yellow bruise remaining.

Whenever it rained we took refuge in the shuttle. Once I tried taking a bibbling in with me, but the bird panicked and beat its wings so furiously against the bulkhead I thought it would kill itself. Adam caught the frightened creature and put it outside.

On one rainy day we were all stretched out lazily, each one of us taking up two seats in the twelve-passenger shuttle. I was playing footsy with Adam across the aisle and enjoying the sound of the rain beating against the shuttle when Justin asked Alison how she happened to join the Diplomatic Corps.

"I kind of came in through the back door," she said. "So did Ben. We were at Pythia—in fact, that's where we met."

"The research colony?"

"That's the one. A barren, ugly world with an artificial environment constructed just for the conducting of medical research. So if somebody in the chemistry lab blew us all up, nobody else would get hurt."

"You didn't like it."

"We did at first. It was exciting, having *all* the equipment you needed and as much help as you asked for. And we had a great deal of freedom to do what we liked—"

Ben: "Within limits."

"Oh, sure, within limits. But we had more freedom at Pythia than we would have had anywhere else."

"So what went wrong?" asked Justin.

"I guess we were just too successful," said Alison, "pardon my immodesty. We found ourselves sitting behind desks thinking up projects for other people to carry out. More and more of our time was spent on administrative work." She laughed. "Then one day Ben said to me, 'You know, if we're not careful, we're going to end up running this place.'"

"So you were ripe for the picking."

"Oh wow, were we. Ben and I aren't administrators, but every day we were getting just a little farther away from the laboratory. So when the Culloden invited us to visit Corps Headquarters, we jumped at the chance. There was this little problem, he said, on a new member world called Kylus. Seems the Kylusians were experiencing an unusually high incidence of dwarf births. Since we'd both done some work with DNA, would we be willing to look into the problem for him? We would. So the Culloden introduced us to our team leader, a tall woman with a baritone voice—"

"Contralto," I murmured.

"—and we quickly became friends. She told us to keep an eye on the pilot who'd been assigned to our mission—she'd decided to marry him but hadn't yet figured out a way to break the news to him."

Adam snorted.

"The Kylusian problem was a challenge," Alison reminisced. "Their DNA is interesting—quite different from ours. But eventually we figured out the proper places on the chain to introduce repressor molecules and made our recommendation to Culloden. That put an end to the dwarf births. By then Adam had broken down and said yes, and Ben and I decided we were better off with the Corps than at Pythia. We've been together ever since."

"When did you join the team?" Justin asked Sondra.

"The next year," she said. "That was over eleven years ago. Eleven years—ye gods. It seems like a hundred."

"Thank you very much," I said.

It was two weeks before Alison pronounced us all "operational" again. Adam was the last to regain his full strength—because he had been the only one to endure the disease without the damping effect of alcohol. Next stop: Lodon, fully recovered from its time of weakness. We hoped. The Whitfields were more interested in trying to find out why Justin was the only one of us to be immune to the disease, but I told them that could wait until after we'd made contact with Commander Zizzi again.

We took the shuttle and made several low passes over the Lodonite army camp. It still wasn't the model of military efficiency the Kamarian camp had been, but it was getting there. The scanners showed us soldiers going about their work in an orderly manner, animals being tended to, supply wagons being loaded. It was safe.

Adam touched down at the eastern edge of the camp. We waited only ten minutes before an armed squad approached us, led by Commander Zizzi. His grizzled beard was gone, and he wore clothing as close to being luxurious as anything we'd seen on this planet. Quite a change from the first time we saw him. He was carrying a bibbling crooked in his arm. His badge of sanity.

The squad stopped and Zizzi took the initiative. "I am Zizzi," he said, "Commander of the Lodonite army. To our offworld visitors, I offer greetings."

His little speech told us two things. First, Zizzi was smooth and formal as opposed to Fluth with his rough-diamond personality. Second, he didn't remember having met us before.

Adam and I introduced ourselves and went through the motions of treating this as our first visit instead of our second. We explained where we were from, why we were in Lodon, and—before Zizzi could ask—that we were unarmed.

Zizzi was sharp. "We are flattered at the Federation's interest in us after so many years. But we speak of that later, yes?"

"That is our hope, Commander," Adam said.

"You arrive at a good time, mirhilancthon," Zizzi responded. "We will have time in which to talk." He meant they were just beginning their time of strength.

I introduced the Whitfields. Zizzi spoke easily to them, displaying more curiosity than all the Kamarians put together. He was especially interested to learn both Alison and Ben were "healers."

Adam: "Commander, may I present Sondra Bark and Justin Bark?"

Zizzi said, "A pleasure, mirhiliptha, mirhilaves."

That was the second time.

The look on Justin's face told Zizzi something was wrong. Adam quickly explained that Justin was a *mirhilancthon* and not a *mirhilaves*.

At that, the three or four soldiers within earshot looked just as stunned as Fluth's soldiers had looked. But unlike Commander Fluth, Zizzi kept his poise. "Forgive my foolish mistake—I apologize, mirhilancthon Bark. Now, may I escort you to our camp?"

Justin mouthed *why me?* at the sky and fell in behind Commander Zizzi as we made our way to the Lodonite camp.

13

The Lodonite camp now looked more like what an army camp should look like. Not all the wreckage left over from the time of weakness had been cleared away, but in general things were well under control. I asked the Commander about the neuters.

"Most of them have returned to their villages," Zizzi said. "They assume responsibility for supplying the army while the rest of us fight in the mountains."

"Sounds as if you depend heavily upon your neuters."

"Yes, we do," he said simply. "More than most people are willing to admit."

That struck me as an odd thing to say, but it was too soon to try to pin Zizzi down. So many questions we needed answers to! But it was always better to let the host set the pace.

Sondra and Justin were watching a group of young soldiers being instructed in the art of knife-fighting. Alison and Ben had *both* wandered off. Adam and I followed Zizzi on his rounds, watching a commander command.

"Ah, here is someone I want you to meet," Zizzi said. "Garrinel? Come over here, please." Our young water-carrier. "This is my *bolaves*." *Bolaves*: Lodonite for "neuter offspring," a nonsexual equivalent of "son" or "daughter."

Garrinel shifted uneasily from one foot to the other and muttered something about being happy to meet us. So the young neuter hadn't mentioned our previous visit.

Adam gave me a surreptitious wink and began asking the Commander how he moved supplies over such rough terrain. They walked a little apart, leaving me with Garrinel.

"You didn't tell him?" I asked quickly.

Head-shake. "I, I tried to. But I couldn't, mirhiliptha. I just couldn't. It would . . . it would have shamed him."

More than you know, kid, I thought. Commander Zizzi would be deeply humiliated to learn he'd once masturbated in front of us. I was determined he'd never find out.

Garrinel was looking *very* uncomfortable. "I didn't know what to do."

"You did exactly the right thing," I reassured the young neuter. "Don't worry about it, Garrinel—I'm glad you didn't tell him. It's easier for all of us if your father doesn't know we were here once before. But we talked to a couple of other people in the camp—they were pushing a soup kettle . . . ."

"Fross and Winna," Garrinel said in a rush. "My friends. They have gone back to their village now. I made them promise to say nothing to my father."

Smart kid. "Garrinel, you're every bit as sharp as your father. Well, I'm glad that's taken care of. We just won't mention it again."

Just then one of Zizzi's officers came up to him and Adam wandered back to Garrinel and me. He asked the youngster, "Are you Commander Zizzi's only child?"

"No, mirhilancthon. My older sister, Kelia, lives in a village to the north, and my younger sister, Weblan, is in the school this year. I had a brother, but the Kamarians killed him."

Adam's eyes narrowed. "What was your brother's name?"

"Bithor."

Adam told me later that was what Zizzi had called him last time, while he was singing the Commander to sleep.

We stayed on in the camp the rest of that day and the two following days. Zizzi courteously insisted we take all our meals with him, and Ben's food analyzer finally found a species of fowl we could eat with no ill effects. The dark gamy flesh took a little getting used to, but we all ended up liking it. Zizzi's mate looked familiar, but I couldn't place her. Alison reminded me: she was the middle-aged woman we'd had to step over in the doorway to enter the headquarters building the first time we'd visited Lodon.

The Lodonites in their sane state were a more sophisticated people than the Kamarians. Zizzi was aware of the existence of things beyond what he could see and touch; Commander Fluth lived completely in the here-and-now. The Lodonites were curious about us, but not as curious as they were about the Kamarians.

They knew we'd been to Kamaria and shot one question after another at us. How many neuter troops did the Kamarians have? Had they developed any new weapons? Were their supply roads in good repair? To all these questions we answered that such information had not been made available to us. Adam did tell them about a new climbing net the Kamarians had developed for scaling exposed rockfaces. The Lodonites were all eyes as Justin innocently sketched a picture of the net he'd "seen" the Kamarians use.

"The Kamarians don't seem to know how the war started," I said to Zizzi during one meal. "They simply say, 'It has always been so.' "

Commander Zizzi made a contemptuous gesture of dismissal. "The Kamarians have no sense of history. They are like animals, following their seasonal instincts, never differentiating one year from another. We don't take many prisoners, mirhiliptha, but those I've talked to were so poorly informed they thought the bibblings have always been here."

We all stopped eating and looked at him.

Zizzi laughed softly. "Ah, you thought so too? Do not listen to Kamarians, my friends. Their heads are stuffed with nonsense." He took a sip of water. "The bibblings have been with us for eight generations. You thought it was longer, yes? Before that, they lived in the northern islands. But something went wrong—the islands grew cold or the food became scarce. So the bibblings left the islands. They came to us first, to Lodon. They belong to us."

Justin: "When did you start fighting the Kamarians?"

"Not until several years after the bibblings first arrived. It took that long for us to understand that our time of strength depended upon the bibblings' presence in our country." Commander Zizzi's face clouded over. "I often think of my ancestors during that first time. That *first* time of weakness. How frightened they must have been! And then to have it happen again, the very next year— without knowing why! It must have been overwhelming, realizing this was going to be the pattern of their lives forever. Strength and well-being when the bibblings were with them, chaos when they were not. A dreadful truth to have thrust upon you."

He roused himself from his painful reverie and went on, "Then one year the Kamarians simply followed the bibblings when they migrated to us. They came armed, swarming through the mountain passes, determined to take over Lodon. We fought them. We fought them all the way back to the mountains. And we have been fighting them in the mountains ever since."

"So the Lodonites have no desire to take over Kamaria?" I asked. "You don't want to follow the bibblings yourselves?"

Zizzi looked at me a moment before answering. "Of course we want to follow the bibblings," he said quietly. "Yes, we want to be sane and healthy all year round. We want to live in peace with our neighbors across the mountains and from across the skies. We want to be able to send our children to school for more than two or three years before we pull them out and teach them to kill. We want a life that isn't all sickness and war. Yes, we would follow the bibblings into Kamaria if we could. The bibblings are our only hope."

There was nothing any of us could say to that. The Commander's dignified and realistic acceptance of an intolerable situation was something we had to respect. Zizzi was a courtly old warrior who had long since come to terms with the impossible life he was forced to lead. I wondered if any of us could have handled the situation as well.

Ben and Alison wanted to run some tests on Justin, to try to find out why he alone of us was disease-proof. Sondra and Adam and I took the opportunity to revisit the village we'd helped save from burning down.

We stood in the narrow street where we'd fought the fire, surrounded by the bustle busy people make when they have things to do. And children! Dozens of them— healthy, normal, underfoot.

Adam: "Cheers and rejoicing, that's one question answered. The young'uns are protected during the time of weakness. Somehow. Somewhere. By someone."

Most of the men had shaved the beards that had grown untended during the time of weakness, so once again we would have trouble distinguishing the neuters from the others. The people we passed seemed content. Understandable. Bibblings everywhere, and the Lodonites themselves at the beginning of a long period of sanity and strength. They'd put the horrors of the last few months firmly behind them.

We openly eavesdropped on a conversation between two farmers. The younger of the two was complaining that the soil in one of his fields didn't smell right and he was asking the older man for advice. Things were indeed getting back to normal.

Some signs of the fire were still in evidence, but most of the damaged buildings had already been painted over with a gray wash of some kind. One building stood out like a sore thumb: a bright-yellow facade smiled out at the street, the work of some Lodonite optimist still trying to bring a little color into a drab life.

Suddenly Sondra poked me and said, "Isn't that . . . ?"

It was the young girl we'd tried to "rescue." The last time we'd seen her she'd been on her back in the street, screaming and twisting in an obscene parody of love. Now we were looking at a bright-eyed, sturdy young thing straight out of Courbet.

"Let me," said Sondra.

Adam and I waited while Sondra went over and made the girl's acquaintance. The girl had long brown hair she kept tossing back while she talked—she was proud of her looks. From the easy way the two were chatting it was clear the girl did not remember Sondra. Sondra brought her over to Adam and me.

"This is Rinta," Sondra said, "and she's just had some good news."

"I'm pregnant!" Rinta blurted out happily.

We offered congratulations as heartily as we could. *Every new life a buffer against extinction.*

Adam: "How old are you, Rinta?"

"Fourteen, mirhilancthon."

"When is your baby due?"

"Shortly before the end of the time of strength. I was luckier this time."

Sondra and I glanced at each other. "*This* time?"

"My other baby was born after the time of weakness had begun." Rinta paused. "He died."

The four of us stood silent for a moment. What was it like, giving birth in the midst of all that madness? That poor baby must have died horribly.

"Perhaps it will be a neuter this time," I said encouragingly.

Extraordinary thing: in a wink Rinta's friendly face froze into a hard mask. "Why do you say that?" she asked in a tight, high voice. She backed off a step from us.

I was astonished at her reaction. "Have I offended you? I'm sorry. I intended no insult, Rinta. I simply thought you'd be happy to have a child who'd remain strong even during the time of weakness."

"Thank you," she said stiffly, and turned her back and walked away.

We stared after her stupidly. "What do you make of that?" I said.

"I'd say young Rinta doesn't want a neuter child," Adam grunted. "And from that appallingly obvious conclusion, another question raises its ugly little head. Is it just Rinta, or do other Lodonite women feel that bearing neuter children is an activity unworthy of their talents?"

"Well," I said, "since keeping the race alive is an urgent matter and neuters don't help a whole lot in that direction—"

"No," Sondra interrupted. "It's more than that. These people resent their neuters, I'm sure of it. I thought as much in Kamaria, but now I'm sure. Don't you remember what Commander Fluth said when he told us that grisly story about the Lodonites baiting a trap with one of their own babies? He said it was 'only' a neuter."

I remembered. "You'd think the neuters would be the aristocracy, wouldn't you? They're the ones who assure the survival of the race during the time of weakness. I don't like all this guessing we're having to do. Let's talk to some of the other women."

Like their Kamarian counterparts, Lodonite women too were worn down from the double duties of childbearing and fighting, giving life and taking it away. But a spark of curiosity flickered in every one of them we talked to: some wish for vicarious release from the drudgery of their lives? For every question of ours they answered, we had to answer two of theirs. But we picked up a few bits of information.

It seemed that almost all Lodonite offspring were conceived during the time of weakness, and that meant very few Lodonite children knew who their real fathers were. The father of Rinta's child could have been any one of the four men we'd tangled with, or the baby could have been conceived even earlier. Some women fought as soldiers during the early months of their pregnancies, and other female soldiers occasionally managed to get through a time of weakness without being impregnated. But to a woman, every Lodonite we talked to looked upon the birth of a neuter child as not quite a disaster, but definitely a disappointment. Some of the women made a show of protesting they would welcome any child born to them—male, female, or neuter. But their protestations didn't quite ring true.

"Think that's why there's no marriage on this world?"

Sondra asked on our way back to the shuttle. " 'Sanctifying' a union to produce legitimate issue is meaningless under circumstances like these. You know, Zizzi might not be Garrinel's father after all. Not his biological father."

"You mean he only thinks he is?" I asked dubiously.

"No, no—none of these people are self-deceived about where the babies come from. Those women were all quite open about the way their children were conceived. Probably a man and a woman pair off during some time of strength, and the man just accepts as his own whatever children the woman might bear. The question of cuckoldry doesn't even enter into it. No Lodonite male is going to consider it 'unmanly' to raise other men's children in his house—since he knows other men are raising his own. It's about as sensible a solution as possible under the circumstances."

Adam: "But it doesn't tell us why the Lodonites and the Kamarians resent their neuters."

"But the resentment itself does explain something else," I said. "It's bothered me for a while—why are both armies headed by men? It would be more logical to put a neuter in charge—someone who's sane all year round."

"And why haven't the neuters ever rebelled?" asked Sondra. "They've been carrying the burden of this maniacal life cycle for eight generations, and yet they're treated like lower-class citizens. Are they so intimidated by their inability to reproduce that they just *accept* whatever the others care to dish out? I don't understand it, I don't understand it at all."

The Whitfields had failed to find an explanation of Justin's immunity to the bibbling disease.

"The tests are superficial, though," Alison said disconsolately, leaning her elbows on the wardroom table. "We don't have the equipment for a really thorough examination. As far as we can tell, Justin's a normal, healthy human being. But then we're all normal, healthy human beings. We added Substance X to a drop of Justin's blood, and nothing happened. It just sat there and stared back up through the microscope at us. The *real* test would be to inject Substance X directly into Justin's bloodstream, but that's a risk we're not willing to take—not even with bibblings flying all over the place. We'll just have to find our answers some other way."

Sondra filled them in on what we'd learned about Lodonite childbearing.

"Wish we had some kind of birthrate stats," Alison mused. "Odd kind of symbiosis. Wonder how it evolved? The bibblings spend twice as much time in Lodon as they do in Kamaria, thus compensating for the Kamarians' topographical advantages. Almost as if nature juggled things in a way to assure perpetual warfare on this planet. Neither side can gain an advantage."

"Unless the cycle's interfered with," said Ben. "If the birthrate of the neuters on one side were to fall, for example, the other side could eventually make enough progress in the mountains to cross over into the other's territory. Now if there were some way of inhibiting the Z chromosome—"

"Now, wait a minute," Justin began.

Ben laughed. "Relax, Justin. Just speculating."

Adam: "But we do have to do something. If we don't come up with something flashy soon, the Culloden's going to start sending us nasty little messages asking how we're enjoying our vacation. It's Himself we have to be thinking of now. Let's at least decide upon some recommendation we can send back."

"I can see three options," I said. "Two of them will take us home immediately, but there are drawbacks. First, we can recommend the Federation take sides in this war —either side will do. Justin likes the Kamarians, I like the Lodonites. Flip a coin. As the Culloden pointed out, once the Federation moves in with its technology, the war will be over in a matter of hours. The Federation won't like that, but if worse comes to worst they can always find some way of rationalizing an aggressive act—they've done it before. But it won't solve the problem of the Lodonites' and the Kamarians' seasonal madness. Remember, the inhabitants of this planet are needed to work the mining operation."

"God, that's coldblooded," said Justin.

"Yes," I said shortly. "Well, what about it? Do we recommend the Federation side with one nation against the other?"

They all said no.

"The second option," I went on, "is to pass the buck. Instead of requesting a Federation pathology team and the whole disease-control operation—which would be an even bigger cop-out on our part, since we know nothing would ever come of it—instead of asking the Federation to come to the disease, we could take Substance X to the Federation. We could simply turn over our samples of the stuff and let Federation laboratories worry about developing a serum."

Ben frowned. "That could take years, Valerie. If it could be done at all. The answer to the disease has to be found here, where the disease originates. Developing a serum would be easy if we just knew how Substance X works. How is a laboratory light-years away from the disease going to find out how it works? I can't see that handing Substance X over to the Federation is going to help the Lodonites and the Kamarians very much."

"It's not going to help *us* very much either," I said. "Technically it would be the proper step to take—we've fulfilled our assignment here. We know why the Lodonites and the Kamarians are fighting and we know what has to be done to stop it. But the simple fulfillment of our assignment just isn't going to be enough this time. Think back to our briefing at Corps Headquarters. Didn't it seem to you that Pilcer and some of the others were coming down even harder than usual with that Anglo-Saxon Invaders stuff? Handwriting-on-the-wall time, folks. *We've got to solve this one ourselves.* Or at least come a hell of a lot closer to it than just handing over a vial of Substance X and saying 'Do something.' "

Justin was shocked. "Let consideration for our careers influence the fate of this planet?"

"That's the way it works." I waited while Justin looked around at the others: he quickly saw we were all in accord on this. Justin still didn't quite believe Culloden would refuse to take action to rid Lodon-Kamaria of its disease if we requested it. And when he saw what he thought was the same sort of coldbloodedness in us, he was shaken. If indeed we were able to solve the disease problem ourselves, the Lodonites and the Kamarians would be a lot better off than if we just dumped the whole mess on the Federation. So there was no quarrel there—it was simply that Justin wanted our motives to be purer than they were. It's always hard when a newcomer learns his profession is not the shiny clean thing he'd like it to be.

We were silent a minute, and then Adam spoke up. "You said three options, Val. What's the third?"

"We form a birdwatching society," I said.

14

We had little trouble in finding out that the bibblings' migration was directed solely by the abundance or scarcity of food. Changes of season were mild on Lodon-Kamaria. The weather was generally temperate year-round on both sides of the mountains; winter here meant rain, not snow and ice. Grubs and insects were plentiful in both lands, but one species of berry that formed an important part of the bibbling diet seemed twice as plentiful in Lodon as in Kamaria. Again, an imbalance in nature that contributed to a balance of military power.

Slightly more trouble: smuggling bibblings back to the ship for Alison and Ben to dissect. The Lodonites valued their golden birds highly—as well they should. We took the shuttle down one night and slipped around in the moonless dark gathering up the unprotesting creatures. Unprotesting, that is, until we popped them into the plastex bags we'd brought with us. Then they beat their wings and made a mewling sound that was incredibly distressing to listen to. The poor things were terrified.

"I feel like a traitor," I growled at Adam. He growled back.

The next morning while Alison and Ben were busy with the bibblings, I sat watching Adam doing pilot things. The ship's orbit was beginning to slip a little, and Adam was putting us back on track. He'd taken control of the ship from the computer and now sat hunched over one of the instrument panels, alternately crooning to the

110

ship and muttering to himself. Sondra and Justin were in their cabin with the door closed.

I read out numbers to Adam until I got bored, and then suddenly made up my mind. "I'm going down to talk to Zizzi again," I announced.

Adam was squinting at a dial showing two wiggly lines. "Why?"

"I think it's time we asked him straight out why the Lodonites don't like their neuters."

"Damned things take forever to align," he grumbled. "I hope you won't put it to him like that."

"Never fear. I shall be circumspect beyond belief."

A burst of bawdy laughter rang out from the Barks' cabin.

"Those rooms must have been designed by an *auditeur*," Adam said absently. "Come *on*." This last to the slowpoke wiggly lines.

"Should I ask about their last attempt at negotiating a truce?"

"Hm?"

"The last attempt at ending the war Fluth told us about. Do you think it's time to ask Zizzi about that?"

"Banzai!" Adam hollered cheerfully and started pulling switches and hitting buttons. Alignment complete.

I sighed and left him to his instrument panel.

The shuttle grew to enormous size when I was the only one in it. I'd never handled a twelve-seater before, but I managed to put down without gouging out too big a hunk of Lodonite terrain. Commander Zizzi was not in his headquarters building and it took me nearly an hour to find him: he was supervising a pack train ready to leave for the mountains. Zizzi was wrapped in a fur-trimmed cloak and was looking rather grand. The man had a dash of dandy in him, and I liked him for it. He must have been something when he was younger.

A bibbling sat on Zizzi's shoulder as he moved among the oxlike animals, inspecting the weapons and trapping equipment. When he caught sight of me, he called out, "Ah, mirhiliptha! One moment, please. I will soon be finished here."

I climbed up on the gate of an animal pen and waited. The pack train was a long one, and a couple of platoons of soldiers were readying themselves to accompany it. I looked off to the mountains. What a lovely world this was! Rich and verdant and full of life and promise. But its most intelligent life form was caught in a vicious struggle just to survive, a struggle that must ultimately prove futile if things went on as they were.

Before long the Commander joined me, and we walked at random through the camp. Zizzi's eyes were never still, darting glances here and there, seeing everything. He made no attempt at small talk, sensing that I had come here for a purpose.

I'd promised Adam I would be circumspect. "The Kamarians say an attempt to negotiate a truce was made in the last generation." So much for circumspection.

"Yes," said Zizzi, "but it failed, unfortunately."

"The Kamarians claim it failed because you used your time of strength to build new weapons after agreeing not to."

The Commander smiled ruefully. "Did they also tell you a similar attempt had been made in the generation before that, and that it was the *Kamarians* who violated the agreement? No, I thought not. We built new weapons last time because we knew from experience the Kamarians were not to be trusted."

Zizzi went on to tell me that attempts to end the war were made periodically. Each new generation would grow desperately sick of the endless killing and sue for peace. Then one side would remember that "last time" the other side had violated the agreement, and the pattern would perpetuate itself. Zizzi said the Kamarians had broken the original agreement, the first time they'd tried to end the war, and the Lodonites could never quite forget that. But now it no longer made any difference. Lodonites and Kamarians alike were locked into a squirrel cage of recrimination and destructiveness.

We'd reached the Commander's headquarters. I invited myself in because I didn't want my next question to be overheard. After we were seated, I said, "Commander

Zizzi, I'd like you to explain something to me. When we first met, you addressed Justin Bark as mirhilaves. Will you tell me why?"

He looked at me as if I were being indelicate. "It was a mistake, mirhiliptha. I did not intend to give offense."

"And none was taken. We just need to understand. Please, Commander—I think it may be important. Why did you think Justin was a neuter?"

Zizzi spread his hands. "He has no odor."

I must have looked as blank as I felt, for he went on to elaborate: "I called him mirhilaves because he emits no male or female odor."

I wasn't sure I was hearing right. "You mean to say you can *smell* the difference among men and women and neuters?"

Commander Zizzi looked interested. "You mean to say that you *can't?*"

The two of us sat there staring at each other in surprise. I was certainly aware of these people's acute sense of smell, but the idea of distinguishing sex by smell—well, that was going to take a little getting used to.

"How do you tell one gender from another?" Zizzi asked, intrigued.

"By appearance. We have no neuters in our race, and we identify men and women by their secondary sexual characteristics—breasts in women, heavy facial hair in men, that sort of thing."

"And are all of your women full-breasted, and do all of your men have heavy beards?"

"No," I smiled. "We make mistakes in identification too."

Commander Zizzi again spread his hands, a silent comment on our way of recognizing sexual difference.

Well, well, well. No wonder we'd had so much trouble identifying the neuters. We kept looking for visible physical signs when in fact there were none to speak of. The Lodonites and the Kamarians never had that problem. They just took a good sniff and *knew.* Zizzi's eyes were glistening; he was as bemused by this difference between our races as I was.

"Thank you for explaining," I said. "That clears up quite a few things I was wondering about."

The old man smiled. "But that's not the real reason you came to talk to me, is it?"

I sighed. "Commander Zizzi, this is what I do for a living. I go from planet to planet, talking to strangers, trying to understand ways of life different from my own. I'm supposed to be good at it. It's a bit disconcerting to find out how easily I can be seen through."

He threw back his head and laughed—the first full-throated laugh I'd ever heard from him. "I don't think you need worry, mirhiliptha. Openness and transparency aren't always the same thing. Besides, you're part of a very effective team—you and the mirhilancthon Chester complement each other quite effectively."

"Yes," I said brightly.

"Professionally, I mean."

"Yes," I said soberly.

It was still the most personal thing he'd ever said to me, and we both welcomed an interruption that gave us time to readjust our bearings a little. Zizzi's mate came in with a sort of herbal tea; I'd tried it before and didn't like it much but drank it anyway.

When the woman had left, Zizzi sipped his tea and looked at me, saying nothing.

"It's about the neuters," I started tentatively. "It may be that I'm totally misinterpreting a situation and I'd like you to set me straight if I am. It seems to me there's a certain . . . resentment of the neuters here. Both here in Lodon and in Kamaria. As if the neuters were merely tolerated instead of being accepted fully by the rest of society. As if they were somehow not quite legitimate. Am I mistaken? Am I seeing things wrong?"

Commander Zizzi seemed to grow even older as I was speaking. "No, you are not mistaken," he said quietly.

"Is it because they can't reproduce?"

He lifted his shoulders a couple of inches and let them fall. "A little. But only among the more ignorant people. The rest of us understand how much we owe our neuters.

The Kamarians would have taken over generations ago if it weren't for our neuters. We would starve during the time of weakness if it weren't for our neuters. We would not even *be* here—if it weren't for our neuters."

"Then *why*?" I said in frustration. "The neuters would be kings on my world. They—"

"What are kings?" Zizzi asked. I'd slipped in the English word without noticing.

"Rulers, people in charge. Uh, commanders."

He nodded.

"But the point is, are we that different from the Lodonites? We would *honor* the neuters instead of merely tolerating them."

"Would you?" Zizzi smiled wryly. "How can I explain—it's very difficult." He stopped to think for a moment. "Have you ever been deeply in debt, mirhiliptha? Not in the sense of owing material things, but in things of the mind." No Lodonite word for "psychologically." "Have you ever owed someone *so much* that you knew you could never in your entire lifetime adequately repay that person?"

"No," I said, "but I've known someone in that position."

"A friend?"

"A relative, as a matter of fact. My father's sister."

"And your relative, how did she feel toward the person she owed so much to?"

"Grateful, of course."

"Of course. Grateful. Nothing else?"

I was beginning to see what he was getting at. "Well, a couple of times I got the impression she was getting a little tired of having to feel grateful."

"Of *having* to feel grateful, yes. We are somehow inadequate if we do not show gratitude where it's due—and that is right, that's as it should be. A beast recognizes no such obligation. A man does. Your relative knew this and felt properly grateful. And went on feeling grateful—for a long period of time?"

"Yes."

"Until her gratitude became a chore? More a duty she must perform than a genuine expression of her feeling?"

I tried to remember some of the things my aunt had said. "I'm not sure. It may have become a duty."

Zizzi nodded. "Perhaps her gratitude was beginning to change into something else? Into resentment?"

I thought this over. "You're saying the Lodonite men and women resent the neuters because they're tired of having to feel grateful to them all the time."

He nodded slowly. "Gratitude can be a *terrible* burden. Can you put yourself in our position, mirhiliptha? Knowing your very existence depends totally upon one group of people and what they are willing to do for you? Knowing that their good will is all that keeps you from extinction?" Zizzi shook his head sadly. "The neuters should be, ah, kings. We should cover them with honors, bow down to them . . . but we don't. We've had to feel too grateful for too long. *And we know the obligation will never be lifted.* Never. Our ancestors lived with that burden of gratitude, and our descendants will live with it as well."

The old man fell into a brown study. I said nothing, waiting until he pulled himself out of it. "People can owe only so much," he said darkly. "There's a limit to how much gratitude they can feel. Pass a certain point and they start resisting. Yes, we resent our neuters, and for that very reason. And it shames me."

I didn't want to ask the question in my mind, but I knew if I didn't ask it now I never would. "Commander Zizzi, does anyone ever resent them enough to kill them?"

He was appalled that I should say such a thing, and made no attempt to hide it. He stared at me tight-lipped, not speaking.

"You told us once not to listen to Kamarians, that their heads were stuffed with nonsense," I said. "I think that was probably good advice. But Commander Fluth told us a story we can't just sweep under the rug. I want you to tell me he's a liar."

"Fluth?" Zizzi mused a moment. "Do you know, I have never seen the man? And I've heard almost nothing about him. But he is a Kamarian, and Kamarians lie as easily as they breathe. What is the story?"

I repeated what Fluth had told us about the Lodonites baiting a trap with one of their neuter babies.

And immediately wished I hadn't. Zizzi's face crumbled and he dropped his chin on to his chest. This man had learned to live with the combined atrocities of war and periodic insanity—but he could still grieve the loss of a baby.

"Then it's true?" I asked, subdued.

Zizzi raised his head. "It could be true. I'd hoped . . . it has been done, in the past. A woman soldier gives birth in the mountains, sees she has produced a neuter, and willingly gives the baby up. Or she dies in childbirth and the child is taken by others. I thought we were past that, now. My grandfather spoke of such things . . . I'd hoped such barbarity was behind us. When did Fluth say this happened? In the present generation?"

"Yes. He said he was on the expedition himself—the one that found the baby. And the trap."

"All I can tell you, mirhiliptha, is that such things have been known to happen. I do not know if Commander Fluth's story is true or not. It's the kind of savagery one expects of Kamarians but finds hard to accept in one's own people. Oh, yes," he smiled when I looked dubious, "the Kamarians have done it—on at least two occasions I know of. The last was—oh, fifteen years ago. The Kamarians are not so pure as they would have you believe."

"Fluth said nothing about his own people. . . ."

"Of course he didn't. To give him more benefit of the doubt than I think he deserves, he might not even know about it. No more than I knew of this incident until you told me. In the mountains . . . have you seen the fighting, mirhiliptha? Have you been in the mountains?"

"Justin Bark has. The rest of us have just flown over in the shuttle."

"People behave differently in the mountains, fighting the war. Normal rules of behavior get forgotten. Women who abandon neuter babies in the heat of war would never think of doing such a thing in their own villages.

It's possible that word of neuter Kamarian babies being used to bait traps never reached Fluth. *We* knew about it, of course—we found the traps. No one knows how much of this sort of thing goes on, because no one talks about it. Not officially, anyway."

- I didn't know what to say.

"The fact that the Kamarians behave like animals doesn't excuse our doing the same thing," Zizzi went on. "I mention it merely to point out once again that you can't believe what Kamarians want you to believe. They are both ignorant and dishonest, and not to be trusted."

They are not to be trusted. How many times had I heard Commander Fluth say the same thing about the Lodonites? Our diplomatic bag of tricks contained no magic formula for undoing generations of distrust, the kind of distrust that's ground in, under the skin, impervious to all effort to clean it out.

"Commander Zizzi, do *you* want to stop the fighting?"

He didn't hesitate a second. "Yes. It has been the dream of my life to see the end of the war—a dream I now know will never be realized. It happens to all of us, mirhiliptha. When we are young we dream of a life we have never known, a life free of the war and the time of weakness. But all too soon we learn that's just a story to lull children to sleep with—nothing more. We fight because we have no choice. If we stop fighting for even *one* time of strength, the Kamarians will destroy us. We kill in order to live."

I shook my head. "There's got to be a solution."

"There is."

I waited, not quite daring to hope.

"You come to us unarmed, mirhiliptha," Zizzi said, "and with words of peace in your mouths. Words which I believe. But you travel across the sky in a magnificent metal ship, a wonderful thing that makes me understand how little we understand. A people who can build such a ship must also have constructed magnificent weapons."

"Commander—"

"You carry no weapons yourselves, but you must know about them. I don't even have to ask you that. You want to stop the war? Give us a weapon, mirhiliptha. Put into our hands the means of defeating Kamaria and the fighting will end. But only then. That's the way to stop the war, mirhiliptha. The *only* way."

15

Out of their cabin at last: Sondra and Justin Bark, looking insufferably pleased with themselves. Adam was talking to them in the wardroom when I got back.

"Zizzi has asked us to supply Lodon with arms," I said by way of greeting.

Justin and Sondra spoke at the same time. "We can't do that," he said. "We may have to do that," she said.

Adam: "When does he want an answer?"

"Didn't say. Just a polite request, this time. But he meant it."

"Of course he meant it," Adam sighed. "Well, it was bound to come eventually. Sooner or later Fluth would have gotten around to asking too. Zizzi wants some kind of superweapon, I suppose. A Zap-the-Kamarians Special?"

"Something like that."

"Well, I'm sure we could supply him. But damned if I'm ready to settle for that kind of solution."

"What about the bibblings?" I asked. "Did the Whitfields find anything?"

"Coupla bugs," Sondra yawned.

"What kind of bugs?"

"*Strange* bugs."

The walk-around space in the ship's lab was on the skimpy side, so I turned on the communicator and asked Alison and Ben to join us in the wardroom. When they got there I asked them about the "bugs."

"The bibblings carry two tiny bacterialike organisms that are unknown to us," Alison said. "Neither is Substance X. But we think they may be causative organisms—one of them might combine with something in the human body to *produce* Substance X. We're setting up tests now, starting with hormones."

"Why hormones?"

"Because of the similarity between Substance X's chemical structure and that of adrenalin. Adrenalin is a hormone."

"Maybe I can save you some time." I turned to Justin. "Justin, I'm going to ask you a highly personal question and I can't even ask it in private. I apologize ahead of time, but I have to ask. Are you sterile?"

They all looked startled, but it was Justin who recovered first. "Yes, I am. Why?"

"You were addressed as mirhilaves by both the Kamarians and the Lodonites. You were untouched by the disease while the rest of us turned into raving maniacs. Incredible as it seems, you and the neuters must have something in common. Commander Zizzi just now told me he mistook you for a neuter because you emitted no sexual odor."

"*What?!?*" All five.

I turned to the rest of them. "Well, look. Men and women *do* smell different from each other. But in a hygienic society that difference is barely discernible, if at all. And you all know what a highly developed sense of smell these people have—and that may be why, to help them distinguish neuters. The rest of us gave off male or female odors. When Zizzi smelled no sexual odor from Justin, he simply assumed he was a neuter."

"Pheromones?" Ben, with a comes-the-dawn look. "Possible—yes, it's entirely possible! We have vestigial pheromones ourselves. Left over from our pre-speech days when we had to convey information through scent instead of sound."

"Spik Inglish," Sondra commanded. "What are pheromones?"

"Substances secreted by an individual that affect the

physiology of other members of the same species. And their behavior as well. Pheromones are small concentrations of molecules that release all sorts of information. Ever hear of bombykol?"

"Good heavens no." Sondra.

"A powerful sexual attractant—if you're a male moth. Female moths release just one molecule of the stuff and find themselves surrounded by admirers. In fact, the standard method of pest control is to develop pheromone suppressants. Cut down the sexual invitations and you limit the insect population. But pheromones aren't just sex-related. In insects and animals they're ways of marking territory, of warning of danger, of laying trails, of identifying members of the family. And of identifying Lodonite and Kamarian neuter humans, it would seem. But that would be a sex-related one."

"You said we had *vestigial* pheromones," Adam said. "Meaning we don't use them any more? That's not true of the people here."

"Most human pheromones are vestigial," said Ben, "but a few are still active. Tracking animals can differentiate human individuals by their scent—we're sending out *some* kind of signal. Schizophrenics have a very special odor in their sweat, caused by one of the hexanoic acids—which does *not* affect the perspiration of nonschizoid people. Now there's a message for you, loud and clear—*help me*. The Lodonites and the Kamarians must have more active pheromones than we do—"

"No," interrupted Alison excitedly, "that can't be right. Zizzi wouldn't have been able to smell male or female messages from *any* of us if our necessary pheromones were merely vestigial. It's not our pheromones that have decayed—it's our *sense of smell!*"

Ben stared at her a moment and then gave an ear-shattering yell and swooped Alison up in a bear hug. They laughed boisterously and hugged each other and did a little dance around the wardroom.

I looked at Adam and lazily raised an eyebrow. "Big Scientific Discovery?"

" 'Twould appear so," he drawled, lowering his eyelids.

"How very nice for all of us," said Justin.

"Charming," said Sondra.

"You four are infuriating," Alison laughed. "We may have just learned something important about ourselves and you sit there oh-so-smug as if you knew it all along!"

Ben, serious again: "Still just a theory. Some evidence, but no proof. But if our bodies do have pheromones sending out unsmelled messages—why, the possibilities are virtually endless! Think of the difference it would make in, say, criminology—if we could learn to identify odors revealing violent intent or unreasoning greed or—"

Come back, Ben. "Could those possibilities include a cure for the bibbling disease by any chance?" I asked.

He thought a minute. "Don't see how. The Lodonite-Kamarian sense of smell and the disease and the Z chromosome and pheromones might all be part of the same package, but the pheromones are just message carriers. Justin, do you know why you're sterile? It's *got* to be a hormone deficiency."

"Not enough testosterone," Justin said. "I've been geting treatment that takes care of the secondary traits, but I can't father children yet."

"Testosterone!" breathed Alison, and looked quickly at Ben. The two of them hurried back to the lab.

"In a way," I said to the others, "you can see how Zizzi might mistake one of us for a neuter. He's not used to relying on the evidence of his eyes—he's been making sexual identifications by scent all his life. And he doesn't really know what offworlders are supposed to look like anyway. We can look at a man and know he's a man, but it's not that easy for the people here. Remember how much alike all three genders look—they dress alike, they all wear their hair any old which way. The men aren't necessarily bigger than the women. The only visual indicator of sex we can rely on is the beard—and most of the men are clean-shaven during the time of strength. The fact that *we* look different from each other—I mean the men look different from the women—well, that probably doesn't mean a whole lot to Lodonites and Kamarians.

They'd still rely on their sense of smell to tell them which was which."

Sondra: "Especially when their neuters look so much like their own boys."

"Their own girls," corrected Justin with a grin.

Adam: "Something else. Both Lodonites and Kamarians are medically primitive—not far from the chicken-feathers-and-eye-of-newt stage, I'd guess. They probably assume all men are fertile, just as all neuters are sexless and unable to reproduce. And since most of the conceiving takes place during the time of weakness—an admittedly questionable label in this context—how are they to know if a man is sterile? These men don't know which children are theirs. There's no way to check up! I doubt if it's ever occurred to them that a man might be sterile and sexually active at the same time."

Something about that bothered me. "Wait a minute—that can't be." I thought a minute. "Wouldn't sterile Lodonites also fail to emit a sexual odor? Couldn't they be identified that way?"

Adam grunted. "Didn't think of that."

Justin: "Maybe not. If their sterility isn't caused by hormone deficiency—if it's something like double-headed sperm, for instance. They'd still have a sexual odor, since the odor seems to depend on hormones."

Sondra nodded. "That makes sense. But it doesn't explain those men who *do* have hormone deficiencies. I can't believe there's not one single man on that entire planet with a hormone deficiency! There must be some. Where do they fit into the scheme of things?"

"The others probably regard them as anomalies that can't be explained by any of the rules they know," I said. "I wonder how such men are treated?"

"Treated how?"

"Socially, I mean. How they're looked on by other men and the women." I repeated Commander Zizzi's explanation of why the neuters were resented on Lodon-Kamaria.

"Gratitude, huh?" Justin, sadly. "What a shame. I guess gratitude would have to be a burden after eight generations. Even eight years is a long time to go on feeling grateful to somebody. What a position for the neuters to be in! They're blessed because they don't get the disease. And they're damned because they don't get the disease."

It was Sisyphusville, all right. In addition to being looked down upon, the neuter spent their lives at a kind of futile labor. Every time they managed to pull their countrymen through another time of weakness, they did so knowing their work would all be undone with the next flight of the bibblings. Bibblings! Such gentle creatures to cause such havoc.

"If the neuters on both sides of the mountains were ever to get together," Sondra mused, "they could put an end to both the war *and* the disease. Just by agreeing not to take care of the men and women during the time of weakness. A high price to pay—the death of every male and female on the planet." She saw Justin looking at her dejectedly and smiled. "Of course they could never do it. It would be suicidal. Without the men and women the neuters would die out too, since they can't reproduce themselves. But you know, I'd be surprised if they haven't thought about it. There must have been times when some neuters somewhere simply thought, 'To hell with it all. *Let* the neuters die out—let *everybody* die out—so what? At least I can live out *my* life in peace.' "

"That's gruesome," I shivered.

Sondra nodded agreement. "Want to bet it's never happened?"

I thought about it. "No."

Adam: "The whole thing's pitiful. Lodon and Kamaria both have let their resentment of the neuters interfere with their own best interests. Maybe neither side has a neuter who would make as good a commander as Zizzi or Fluth, but it *has* to be to their advantage to have a rational mind in charge all year round. Zizzi should be training Garrinel to take over—but Garrinel will just go on carrying water and doing other donkey work. Pitiful."

"I've been wondering," said Justin. "Why don't the Kamarians just plant more berry bushes? Do you think they don't know that's why the bibblings spend more time in

Lodon? They must have made the connection between migration and the search for food."

I leaned my head on Adam's shoulder and closed my eyes, listening to Justin talking about berry bushes, filling in the time until Alison and Ben could come up with something. I was just beginning to realize how lucky we were to have Justin Bark with us. Not only because he'd saved us from the disease, but that too—he'd kept his head in an extreme emergency and had known exactly what to do. And had done it. But even more than that: we were lucky to have him because of what he himself was. An irony we could have done without: Justin, with all his supermale traits, was considered not quite masculine by the inhabitants of the first world the Diplomatic Corps sent him to. He'd taken that slap in the face with annoyance but nothing more: he'd not made an issue of it. And he'd endured our discussion of his sterility without seeing *that* as a threat to his manhood. Justin was still green as a diplomat, but as a man he was all the way home.

We had been right to trust Sondra's judgment.

"Got it!" Shiny-eyed Alison, lighting up the wardroom. "One of the two organisms the bibblings carry combines with certain hormones—testosterone in males, estrogen in females—to produce Substance X. And the other organism—are you ready?—combines with the *same* hormones to produce 'anti-X'—the antidote!"

All of us sophisticated types burst out cheering like a bunch of kids. Light at the end of the tunnel! The silver lining on the cloud! Hope trapped in Pandora's box! (Well, no, that doesn't quite fit, but what the hell.) For the first time since we came to this wretched-beautiful planet, we were on top of things.

When the excitement died down some, Alison continued: "The anti-X causes Substance X to break down and pass harmlessly out of the body. The neuters, of course, have no testosterone or estrogen in their bodies, so they are unaffected by either organism. Both organisms simply pass through their bodies, combining with nothing along the way. Justin's testosterone deficiency protected him the same way."

We all made a big show of congratulating Justin for having the foresight to bring along a built-in immunity when visiting a diseased planet. He laughed until his eyes watered. We were all feeling so good we would have laughed at anything.

Adam somehow managed to laugh and look puzzled at the same time. "Why is there any disease at all?" he finally asked. "Why don't the two organisms just cancel each other out?"

"The anti-X organism is faster-acting and shorter-lived than the X-causing one," Ben explained. "Remember how quickly we all recovered once Justin exposed us to the bibblings? It was just a few days. We think the X-causing organism goes through a long latent period. It's left behind after the birds migrate, probably in their droppings. The droppings dehydrate, the organism becomes airborne and is taken into the body through inhalation. By then all the anti-X organisms left behind have expired. With no bibblings around to provide a continuing supply of the counteracting organism, the disease progresses unchecked."

I asked. "What about a vaccine, Ben?"

"Shouldn't be a problem, now that we know how the disease works. Right now we need about ten hours' sleep—"

"At least," murmured Alison.

"—and then we'll start on it. We'd make too many mistakes if we tried it now. We were working on this thing all last night and today."

"This vaccine," I said. "That's for us?"

"That's for us."

"What about the people who already have the disease?"

Ben frowned. "A vaccine wouldn't do the job. You see, what we're going to do is use the anti-X organism and hormone combination to kill the X organism, which we'll then put in a suspension. That'll give us immunity against contagion by counteracting the *un*modified organism. But it won't do anything to fight any fully developed Substance X already in the bloodstream—we'd need a serum of straight anti-X organisms for that."

"But you could make such a serum," I said.

"Yes, of course."

"Then go ahead with it. We—"

"Whoa, Val, hold on. We can't make enough serum in that little lab to bring a whole nation back to health."

"I know you can't. Just make enough for one person."

"*One* person?"

"That's right," I said. "Once we're all inoculated, we've got to go back into Kamaria and kidnap Commander Fluth."

16

She was watching a creepy-crawly work its way across the open barn door with a concentration usually found only in entomologists. She was Kamarian, about six or seven years old, and totally untouched by the bibbling disease. The bug disappeared into a crack in the wall and the little girl scampered away looking for other amusement.

"That," I said positively to Adam, "was not a neuter. Nobody is going to make me believe that was a neuter. That was a little girl."

Adam: "No argument."

Next to me Alison nodded. "She's a girl, all right. A healthy little girl."

The only healthy non-neuter Kamarian we'd seen. "How come?" I asked.

Alison: "Sexual immaturity. Her body hasn't started manufacturing estrogen yet. They're all safe from the disease until they reach puberty. So this is where they keep the children during the time of weakness—isolated somewhere out in the country. Must be hundreds of places like this. One more job for the neuters—babysitting."

We were inside the barn, resting and taking stock of our situation. It had taken Ben and Alison four days to develop a vaccine they could agree on. When the five susceptible members of the team were safely inoculated, we'd put down in Kamaria and approached the army camp cautiously.

It was Lodon all over again: Kamaria's military spit-and-polish had degenerated into a shambles, the soldiers either drunk and sleeping or awake and fighting mad. The ones not yet sleeping lurched along in gangs—large, reeling forms straight out of Pieter Brueghel. We made a slow progress through the camp; Justin would scout ahead and then come back for us when he'd found a safe way. Run a bit, hide a bit, run a bit, hide a bit.

Whoops: orgy in progress. Justin led us into a barracks building that had been empty a few minutes ago but now was busy busy busy. On the floor: six or seven men and women entwined in a moving tangle of arms and legs and clothing like a multiheaded creature doing its daily exercises. The, ah, *orgiasts* looked up when we walked in and one woman actually smiled at us, as unself-conscious as a Cranach nude. We beat a hasty retreat.

Outside a new fight was breaking out. Justin checked the next barracks and motioned us over. We all ran for the open door, which Justin barred as soon as we were all inside.

"Is all that caused by the disease?" I asked, sinking down on some absent soldier's straw mattress. "Are they *in heat* as well as everything else that's wrong?"

"Could be," Ben puffed, leaning against the wall. "Their hormonal balance is all out of whack, no doubt. Maybe the women's estradiol supply is up. If so, they'd start elaborating short-range aliphatic compounds in response—and that would be enough to get the men going."

"You're talking about pheromones again?" Sondra, seeing if she remembered the word right.

"Yes," said Ben. "*This* could be why they've developed such a keen sense of smell—to assure continuation of the species. They have to be prolific to compensate for the numbers claimed on such a regular basis by the war and the disease."

"Would eight generations be long enough for that kind of adaptation?" Alison said dubiously. "More likely they've simply retained an acute sense of smell they've always had."

Adam sat next to me and draped an arm over my

shoulders. I smiled at him and only half-listened to the
Whitfields wrangling gently over whether the Kamarians
had always smelled well or whether they had evolved the
ability to smell well. One thing was certain: right now
they didn't smell *good*. The stench outside was every bit
as overpowering as it had been in the Lodonite camp
when we'd first visited there.

"The fight's over." Justin, listening at the door. He
pulled back the bar and opened the door enough to look
outside. He slipped out for a few minutes and then was
back, saying, "Come on. It's clear now."

We made it all the way to Commander Fluth's headquarters that time—and of course the Commander wasn't
there. Neither was anybody else.

"Where was he the last time we saw him?" asked Sondra. "Right out in front of the building, wasn't he? Dancing up a storm?"

Ben: "Yes, we took a blood sample, I remember. Right
before we came down with the disease ourselves. But he
could be anywhere by now."

"Water carriers and soup servers," said Adam. "Sane
neuters dispensing life to the insane. There've got to be
some around here somewhere. And *we've* got to find
them—they're the only ones here we can talk to."

Like Lodon, Kamaria used neuter adolescents to feed
the maddened populace during the time of weakness. The
fighters, fortunately, seemed to have exhausted themselves. We were able to search for the neuters in safety,
but we all felt uneasy in the camp. I for one would be
glad to get out of there. We finally found one neuter
who'd seen Commander Fluth dance away.

"He took the west road," the young neuter said. "I
tried to stop him—we could take care of him here. But I
couldn't—he was too strong. Out there . . . ," the young
voice trailed away shakily.

Out there, away from the camp and the villages, the
Commander could easily starve to death. "Don't worry," I
told the youngster. "We'll find him."

"I wish I were that sure we would," Sondra muttered
as we tramped back to the shuttle.

We flew west, zigzagging back and forth across the road, scanning the ditches. We looped out over the adjoining fields in case Fluth had wandered away from the road. No sign of him. We touched down at the first village we came to.

The place was totally deserted. The village was almost large enough to be called a small town, so it took the six of us two hours to check every building. Knock knock, who's there, is *anybody* there. All we found was one dead bibbling in a cage—somebody's pitiful attempt to hold onto his sanity. Nothing was burning; there were some signs of breakage, but nothing extraordinary. It was just that everybody had left.

Justin: "They must have taken off right after the bibblings migrated. A village this size would be more dangerous than the smaller ones."

"Westward ho?" asked Adam.

We climbed back into the shuttle and zigzagged our way west to the next village. This one was much smaller and appeared quiet from where we touched down nearby. We hadn't yet reached the main street when a familiar sound reached our ears. *Slap slap slap*. Feet hitting the ground. Dancers.

We edged around the corner of a weaver's shop and saw them, about a dozen men and women doing their eerie, gooseflesh-raising dance of madness. Heads back, eyes glazed, mouths breathing out little flecks of foam. Pump-pump-pump went their knees; elbows flapped like the wings of a flock of flightless birds unaware they were forever grounded. We examined each face carefully: Commander Fluth was not among them.

Something new: behind the dancers came three adult neuters, huddling together nervously, keeping an eye on the dancers. When they caught sight of us they stopped, began backing away.

"It's all right!" I called out. "We're not . . . affected by your time of weakness."

The neuters hesitated. Adam stepped forward and told them who we were and why we were here and had they seen Commander Fluth lately?

One of the neuters nodded. "He was here. Maybe fifteen days ago. I fed him myself." The other two neuters moved off after the dancers. One of them walked with a limp.

"He's gone now?" I asked.

"Yes. I tried to get him to stay with . . ." the neuter gestured after the dancers. "But the Commander is a strong man. I could not make him stay without hurting him." The neuter shrugged disconsolately and started to follow the others. Keepers of the peace.

"Which direction did he go?"

"West," was the answer.

When we reached the shuttle, Sondra said: "We're almost out of daylight. Maybe we ought to start here tomorrow."

"Let's give it one more try," I said. I knew what was worrying her. Nights on Lodon-Kamaria were virtually solid black: no moonlight, almost no starlight. Lodonites and Kamarians carried torches when they had to go out after dark, torches that illuminated the ground for maybe two or three meters in front of their feet. Indoors was even worse: simple lamps, wicks floating in oil, lots of smoke and very little light. No candles. Life on the planet came to a halt when the daylight was gone. We'd all carried small powered lamps on our night hunt for bibblings. But the bibblings had been everywhere; finding them was no problem. Looking for a single crazed man at night in a nation of crazed men was a different matter altogether.

West, the neuter had said: easier said than done this time, as it turned out. Several kilometers west of the village, the road forked. Right or left? Partially harvested fields of bluish-brown grain stretched away north to the beginning of a woods in the distance. To our left lay a group of farm buildings, the only sign of habitation in sight. So we put down again, near the main farm building.

A huge stone building, sprawling in a manner that suggested rooms had been added on to the original structure. So many Lodonite-Kamarian homes were built of stone, in spite of the superabundance of trees on the planet. Better protection during the time of weakness.

We walked all the way around the building, looking for an open door or window and finding none. Adam tried one of the doors. "It's barred on the inside. Somebody's in there." He started to pound on the door and then thought better of it. "Hallo! We won't harm you—we're looking for Commander Fluth! Have you seen him? Hallo?"

No answer.

We tried the other doors and a few of the double-shuttered windows without being able to raise a response. For lack of anything better to do, we decided to go look in the barn. That's when we spotted the little girl watching an insect crawling into the wall.

The child was now picking flowers not far from the barn, oblivious to our presence. "What's she doing out here alone?" Sondra wanted to know. "Does she belong in that locked-up farmhouse?"

"That's it!" Adam said and ran back to the main farm building. Wondering, the rest of us followed.

"Hallo!" Adam said to one of the closed doors. "Are you missing a little girl? About six years old, long brown hair, likes insects . . ."

The door remained closed, but we could hear a bar being slipped back from one of the windows. A thick wooden shutter pushed forward an inch, two inches.

"Oh, there you are," Adam said brightly, speaking to the crack between the shutters. "There's a little girl out here and she seems to be all by herself. We were wondering if that's quite safe? Under the circumstances. Shall we fetch her back?"

The shutter pushed all the way open and a long Modigliani face appeared in the window. "Mitta?" The neuter looked worried.

"Is that her name?" said Adam. "She's quite all right—picking flowers, as a matter of fact."

"That's Mitta," the neuter nodded. "Every day she picks flowers. She did not come when I called, when I saw—" the neuter broke off uncertainly.

"When you saw us coming," Adam finished the sentence. "I do apologize. We didn't mean to startle you. But it's getting dark—we'd better bring Mitta back."

"On my way," said Ben and trotted off toward the barn.

The door didn't open to us until Ben returned with little Mitta riding his shoulders, laughing delightedly the way children should laugh, clutching her small bouquet of wildflowers. The worried-looking neuter let us in and threw open the windows to admit the last of the fast-fading daylight.

We found ourselves in the largest single room we'd seen on Lodon-Kamaria. A number of doorways led to smaller rooms—sleeping cubicles, we later found out. In addition to the worried-looking neuter, about thirty pairs of young eyes were looking at us curiously.

The neuter's name was Glawklug, a nice throatful of gutturals. Glawklug's job was taking care of the children in this isolated spot during the time of weakness. That meant no school for anybody when the bibbling disease was sweeping the land.

"You're the offworlders, aren't you?" Glawklug said softly.

I said we were, and spoke our names.

"I have heard you were here," Glawklug nodded. "They say you ask many questions and hurt nobody."

Not a bad reputation to have. The Whitfields were moving among the children, peering down small throats and gently prodding tummies. "Do you take care of all these children by yourself, Glawklug?" I asked.

"The older children help. They are very good about it."

One of the older children was a fetching young lass of about twelve who had a bad cold. She kept wiping her nose on her sleeve when she thought no one was looking and casting surreptitious glances at Justin. She found some excuse for sidling over in his direction, and soon started talking to him, displaying all the petulant delicacy of a Sienese virgin. Justin, amused, answered her seriously as if she were an adult.

Other children who did not have a cold in the nose were equally amused. Finally one of them slipped up to the girl and whispered something in her ear. The girl turned beet-red and darted from the room to a chorus of giggles. Her friend had obviously told her she'd been flirting with a neuter.

"Better luck next time," Sondra murmured to her husband, who rolled his eyes heavenward.

Dominating the room: a long trestle table. Glawklug and two of the children were laying out the evening meal. Five pieces of cheese, a hunk of stale bread, four pieces of a fruit I didn't recognize, a pot of watery something that might have been stew.

"Is this all you have?" I asked, appalled. "You can't feed thirty children on this!"

"Dunta has not been here for ten days," Glawklug said worriedly. "Tomorrow I must go into the village myself." Dunta, it turned out, was the neuter who brought them supplies every five or six days.

I called Alison over and explained the problem. "Those emergency rations in the shuttle—can the Kamarians assimilate our food?"

"Some of it," she said. "Enough to hold them for a while. The children seem to be in good health. You've taken good care of them, Glawklug."

"We can't take your food, mirhiliptha," Glawklug protested. "You'll have nothing to eat yourselves."

"We're in no immediate danger of wasting away," Alison laughed. "Besides, we can always get more. Go on and take it, Glawklug. Just warn the children the taste will be different from what they're used to."

Night had now fallen, and Adam and I groped our way out to the shuttle and back with our nutritious nongourmet emergency rations. Inside the farmhouse the only light came from the fireplace; no luxuries such as lamps here. Some of the children ate the rations as uncritically as if they'd been eating them all their lives; others were not so happy with the alien taste. I watched Adam coax one suspicious little boy into eating a protein bar by telling him stories about the world it came from.

But the big hit of the evening was Ben Whitfield. The children loved him. They were all over him, touching him, hanging onto his clothes. Ben is a gentle man, but I think his size must have had something to do with it. Here was this big, impressive, male authority figure who'd managed to hold onto all his senses during the time of weakness. The children didn't see many like that.

I waited until Glawklug had the younger children tucked in for the night and asked about Commander Fluth.

"Ten days ago exactly," Glawklug said. "The last time Dunta was here with our supplies. Together we were able to hold him down long enough to feed him and give him some water. But when we tried to put him in the cart so Dunta could take him back to the village . . ."

"I know," I sighed. "He's a strong man. Which way did he go, did you see?"

"He took the north fork of the road. The last time I saw him—" Just then one of the sleeping children began to whimper, and Glawklug hurried off to see what was the matter.

I went over and sat down on the floor next to Sondra, our backs against the wall and our feet stretched out toward the fire. "We've got to find Fluth," she said. "We've got to put an end to this. That poor, harassed neuter trying to take care of all these children alone . . . and Glawklug's not the only one. There are places like this all over the planet. Eight generations of this! I don't see how they stand it."

"They're a remarkable people," I said. "Not only have they stood it all these years, they've managed to retain their humanity as well. Think how well we've been received here. They don't know us—they don't really know what we want. Yet we've been treated courteously on both sides of the mountains. No one's tried to stab us in the back or even steal from us. When was the last time we went on a mission where we didn't have to spend half our time pussyfooting around local political situations that had nothing to do with our reason for being there? No one's tried to *use* us or manipulate us. The only people we've found who qualify as bad guys are those few who use babies to bait traps in the mountains."

Sondra: "They'd probably have their share of villains if their life conditions were closer to what we consider normal. Right now the bulk of everybody's hostility is directed toward the common enemy. But you're right—they're remarkably humane for a people who've never known peace. Maybe that's why they value civilized behavior so highly—because it's so fleeting."

Adam dropped down next to me. "Look over there in the corner."

In the corner at the edge of the flickering firelight, Ben lay sprawled out with four children curled up against him, all five sleeping the sleep of the innocent. Glawklug came back and stopped to look at them and smile. One child had an arm around Ben's neck; another's head and shoulders rested on his chest.

"How trusting children are," Adam said. "Too trusting, in fact. Ben could be a Lodonite spy in disguise for all they know. But their instincts tell them he's a kind man and so they trust him."

Yes, they trusted him. Trust came easily to them. It was only later they'd be taught distrust, learning from the adults that all Lodonites were treacherous, bloodthirsty animals who'd as soon kill them as look at them. And at the same time Lodonite children were being taught the same thing about *them*. It was a vicious cycle *that had to stop*.

And we could stop it. If only we could find Commander Fluth.

17

We found him.

We spent the night in the farmhouse with the children and left at first light the next morning. One little girl burst into tears when she realized Ben was going away. Big Ben: hugging, comforting, finally making her laugh.

"Goodbye, Glawklug," I said, "and the best of luck to you." *To all of you, all the Glawklugs of Lodon-Kamaria.*

"You will help our Commander when you find him, won't you?" Glawklug's long face gazed at me anxiously. The neuter seemed embarrassed.

"Of course we will. That's why we're looking for him. Don't worry."

As Adam lifted the shuttle off, I puzzled over Glawklug's moment of embarrassment and thought I understood it. The neuter had been in the awkward position of asking total strangers for help—strangers who *seemed* to be allies, but nonetheless strangers. Offworlders to whom the shameful time of weakness lay exposed in all its ugliness. It was only natural Glawklug should be embarrassed.

And what about us, cast in the role of saviors? That was embarrassing in itself. But we'd helped cast ourselves: buttinsky know-it-alls who were going to solve this little world's problems for it. God knows they had problems and they *did* need help. And in the Vast Eternal Scheme of Things there was only one way our presumptuous interference could be justified: by success. Unqualified, unmistakable, unparalleled success. *We're not allowed to fail*, I'd told Justin Bark before we started out. So get in there and fight! Go Anglo-Saxon Invaders! Yay team!

Shit.

Adam threw me a concerned look: he always knew when I got in one of those who-the-hell-do-we-think-we-are moods. But he didn't have time to say anything because we were over the north fork of the road and starting our zigzag-and-loop pattern.

It was early enough in the morning that a slight haze still lay over the land. This meant we had to fly lower than we liked, and the search moved a little more slowly than we liked. Sondra was worried that the Commander had wandered off into the woods in the distance; we'd never be able to spot him from the air if he had. After a couple of hours the haze lifted and we were able to fly higher. The north fork ran through an uninhabited part of Kamaria—not even a farmhouse in sight. We zigged and we zagged and we looped until Vayner stood high in the sky.

"There he is," said Adam. "Straight ahead."

Commander Fluth had stayed with the road—perhaps there was something about a continuous line that hypnotized dancers. He'd made it this far along the north fork before he'd collapsed. We found him spread-eagled in the middle of the road, one unshod foot a bloody mess. He was still alive.

The rest of us waited while the Whitfields examined him. "Exhaustion, dehydration, malnutrition, and sunburn," Alison said. "Foot infection. Fractured right fibula. He's been dancing on a broken leg."

The disease-that-never-quit chose that moment to make itself visible once again. Even in his half-dead state Fluth responded to the demands of Substance X: his arms began to twitch, his knees jerked upward in a weak pumping action. His bloody foot flapped helplessly against the ground.

Sondra leaned her head against Justin's arm and closed her eyes. "I don't know how much longer I can go on watching this. Nobody should have to suffer like that. Nobody."

Justin slipped his arm around her. "Just a little longer. The end's in sight."

Adam touched my earlobe. "What about you? Over your blue funk yet?"

"Yes," I said, and realized it was true. Those moods never lasted long. Besides, our feelings were not important compared to Commander Fluth's condition.

Ben carried the Commander to the shuttle and we lifted off. All the way back to the JX-31 Sondra hovered over Fluth, trying to feel his pain for him. Our supersophisticate who loathed underdeveloped worlds had crossed over some invisible line; Sondra had allied herself firmly with the suffering Kamarians and Lodonites. Detachment be hanged.

None of us had eaten for over a day, so the Barks and Adam and I tended to our stomachs while the Whitfields tended to Commander Fluth. They set his leg, treated his infected foot, fed him intravenously. They cleaned him up and dressed him in some of Adam's clothes—Ben's were too big. And, most important, they shot him full of anti-X serum.

"How long?" Adam asked when the Whitfields finally sat down to eat.

Ben: "Can't be certain. It took us three days."

It took Commander Fluth five—he was weaker than we had been and he'd had the disease longer. When at last he struggled to open his gummed-shut eyes, it was to find himself in a spaceship for the first time in his life, orbiting his own planet.

The man's gratitude was heartbreaking. When he understood we had indeed found a way to end the time of weakness, he cried like a child. He became gruff and inarticulate when he tried to thank us. We played the whole thing down, leery of too much gratitude with the example of the neuters before us.

In the privacy of our cabin, Adam said: "Do you feel like a blackmailer? I do. Now that we know the serum works, what possible excuse do we have for not using it? Instead we're going to tell that man out there that we'll cure his countrymen only if he'll do *us* a few minor favors—end the war, join the Federation, sell us mining rights. Little things like that."

"You having second thoughts about asking Culloden to send in medical help?" I asked.

"Second, third, and fourth thoughts. Labor at it as I will, I am utterly unable to persuade myself that the Father of Us All will respond to a cry for help with a humane and altruistic gesture. I know damned well he'll stall." Adam scowled. "So why am I struggling with this irresistible impulse to ask him anyway?"

"That's your unconscious at work—obeying the commands of your instinct for self-preservation," I said sententiously. "I know. I've got the same instinct hammering away at me."

"You've changed your mind?"

I nodded. "I think it may be a tactical error *not* to notify Culloden. If we fail to bring this off, he can always say *but you never let me know you needed help if you had asked I would have et cetera*. I agree he's not going to help the Lodonites and the Kamarians unless they sell their mining rights. But I want it on the record that the failure to help them is Culloden's responsibility and not ours. A formal request for medical assistance would do the trick. Culloden's slippery—he'll find some way to weasel out. But it wouldn't be that easy for us—we'd get burned, and burned bad. If there's going to be any heat, I want *him* to get it."

"I love it when you're nasty," Adam deadpanned.

The light above our cabin door went on. Adam activated the door and Justin Bark stepped in.

"Adam and Valerie," he said formally, "I've come to a decision. We have got to stop this disease regardless of any business arrangement the Federation might make with the Kamarians and the Lodonites. I want you to send a message to Culloden asking for medical assistance." He took a deep breath. "And if you won't contact him, I will. I *insist* he be notified."

"All right," I smiled, and watched his sternness dissolve into surprise.

The six of us talked it over at length and decided to make a full report rather than just request medical assistance. That way the Culloden couldn't claim he didn't have the overall picture—*and* it would show how busy we'd been. Only Justin believed that this report was for the benefit of the Lodonites and the Kamarians; the rest of us knew it was for *us*. Justin simply could not accept the extent of selfish interests at work within the Corps. This was one he was going to have to learn the hard way.

We gave Culloden everything: a full description of the disease—how it worked, what it looked like, how it *felt*. How it caused the war, how the bibblings were responsible, how the Whitfields had developed a serum. How we had the commander of the Kamarian army aboard ship right now, sane once again and on the road to good health. How we needed medical help—lots and lots of it, right away, don't dally, please hurry, yours truly.

Culloden made us wait two full days before he replied. We all crowded around the display screen to watch his answer appear line by line.

Congratulations on a superlative effort! You have far exceeded the Corps' expectations and more than justified my own high opinion of your abilities. All members of the team are being upgraded one rank, with special citations awaiting Dr. Alison Whitfield and Dr. Benjamin Whitfield.

Since the Federation was unaware Lodon-Kamaria is a diseased world, Medical Services are unfortunately not immediately equipped to deal with the problem. All of the Federation's epidemic control teams are en route to the Marmyon star system, where an outbreak of plague has been reported. I am attempting to recall six of the teams and divert them to Lodon-Kamaria. But I do not wish to build false hope. It may be a full Federation-time year before help reaches you. I am sorry; this is the best I can do.

In the interim, you may wish to open negotiations with Commander Fluth. This is not obligatory on your part. You have already fulfilled the goals of your mission (and more), and are free to return to Corps Headquarters anytime you deem fit.

Again, my warmest congratulations.

"That son of a bitch." Justin, stunned.

Sondra: "The lady's not here and can't defend herself."

"That *prick!*"

"That's better."

Nobody said "We told you so"; there was no need. No one believed for one moment that *all* the Federation's epidemic control units were scooting off to Marmyon to fight a plague—maybe a dozen or so, but not all. If there was a plague. And even Justin caught the veiled instruction in Culloden's response: either go to work on Fluth or report back to headquarters immediately.

By the end of the day Justin had slipped into a depression. He refused the medication Alison offered him.

"Let him work his way through it," Sondra said to Alison. "He'll bounce back. He's resilient."

He did bounce back, a couple of days later. But his eyes looked a little narrower, and he didn't seem to smile as easily as he used to.

Now it was just a matter of waiting for Fluth to regain his strength. Soon he was limping about the ship, visibly overwhelmed by so much strangeness all about him. He spent hours at the scanners, seeing his world from a brand-new viewpoint. He was especially fascinated by the sight of the vast pink desert on one of the unsettled continents.

"I never believed those stories about a land of sand," he said softly. "But they're true."

The man's powers of adaptation were remarkable. A very literal-minded, if-I-don't-see-it-I-don't-believe-it person, Commander Fluth. One hundred fifteen days: that's how long we'd been here, that's how long the JX-31 had been in orbit. But not once had Fluth shown the slightest curiosity about the ship: it's up here and he's down there and ne'er the twain shall meet. He thought. But now that the twain *had* met, he accepted the alien environment with the same matter-of-factness with which he approached everything. *Strange, scary, I don't understand it but it's real and it's here so I'll live with it.*

Adam: "Are you comfortable? Do you want anything?"

Fluth: "Can you fix it so I could get a closer look at Lodon?"

The next step was up to me.

I waited until Fluth started alternating complaints that he was now well enough to go back to his war with strongly worded "requests" that we cure the rest of the Kamarians: that was my go signal. I took the shuttle down to the Lodonite army camp.

In Kamaria, Adam was the one we'd sent to work on Fluth, yet I was the one with the most direct line to Zizzi. Odd, in a way: you'd have thought it would be the other way around. Fluth and I were both blunt talkers and should have gotten on like a house afire. Adam and Zizzi, on the other hand, were both subtle and articulate and would have made good partners in crime, so to speak. But Zizzi was amused by my head-on approach to things, and Fluth obviously got a kick out of listening to Adam go on. Well, so be it. People have the damnedest way of *not* running true to form.

Zizzi was in the mountains, and rather than try to find him I decided to wait. Adam could always tell Fluth he couldn't be returned to Kamaria because I'd taken the only ship-to-surface transport. On the third day Zizzi returned, and I gave him another day to rest up and/or do whatever returning commanders do.

He greeted me with a cocked eyebrow. "So the mirhiliptha Chester has not abandoned us after all. I was wondering whether you had returned to Kamaria."

He can't really read minds, I told myself. "We had work to do on the ship, Commander." And other places. "We wouldn't leave without saying good-bye."

"Oh, I knew you hadn't returned to your homes," he smiled. "Your ship still passes by several times a day. A faint speck in the sky, but always there."

Ah yes, the ship. Glad you mentioned it first. "Was your expedition to the mountains successful? Or should I not ask?"

Slight shrug. "We will not know for some time whether our new traps are successful or not. I am satisfied with their placement, yes. And we managed to trip two Kamarian traps without anyone getting hurt."

"Sounds like a very successful expedition," I said. "Are you planning another one soon?"

Zizzi spoke easily of his long-range plans without going into any detail about what kind of trap he planned to set, or where or when. Smart. Knew just how to keep the visiting busybody happy without giving away any real information.

I waited until the conversation began to run down and then played my ace, gambling that the personalities of Fluth and Zizzi were as different as I thought they were. I said that even though the Commander was obviously busy, could he steal some time for a ride in our nice shiny spaceship?

He bit.

18

We didn't make it to the JX-31 immediately, though, for the simple reason that I'd forgotten to allow for the novelty appeal of the shuttle. Zizzi had no way of knowing, of course, but the sensation of flying was much stronger in the shuttle than in the ship; what enchanted the Commander was the close-up bird's-eye view of his native land the shuttle scanners gave him. And never for a minute did he forget his military obligation: he wanted me to fly up and down the mountain range so he could look for Kamarian traps. I pleaded a shortage of fuel (untrue) and eventually docked with the JX-31.

Our plan was for Adam to keep Fluth out of the way until Zizzi had time to get over his initial excitement at seeing the inside of the ship. But after a few hours I was beginning to think that just wasn't going to happen. Zizzi was a glistening-eyed, perpetual-motion question machine. He wanted to know *everything*. He was over twice as old as I was but *I* was the one who ran out of steam. I turned on a communicator and asked Adam to round up the others and meet us in the wardroom.

How To Stage Somebody Else's Moment of Truth. *Scene:* Wardroom of a Federation-owned JX-31. *Chorus:* Six slightly nervous offworlders. *Major antagonists:* Commander Zizzi of Lodon vs. Commander Fluth of Kamaria. *Action:* Confusion.

Our worst fear was that the two men would take one look and leap for each other's throats. A fistfight we

147

weren't worried about, but Zizzi carried a dagger. Fluth, of course, was unarmed. Zizzi was startled at seeing Fluth there, but then looked curious—*and friendly*. I remembered he'd once said he'd never seen Fluth, and what he was looking at now was a stranger wearing alien clothing aboard an alien ship. Presumably another one of us. He didn't know who Fluth was.

But Fluth knew who *he* was. The Kamarian Commander pointed an accusing finger at the older man and said, "You're Zizzi!"

"I know that," Zizzi said pleasantly, "but what I don't know is who you are."

"Fluth," the other spat out. Not "the Supreme High Commander of the Grand and Glorious Kamarian Army" or any other puffery like that. Just the one syllable: *Fluth*.

It was enough. I didn't even see his arm move, but Zizzi's dagger was suddenly in his hand. He threw me an accusing look: "Oh, mirhiliptha!"

Unsaid: *You tricked me! Betrayal!* I felt guilty as hell.

Adam stepped toward the two men—but not between them—and raised a cautionary hand. "Commander Fluth is not armed," he said to Zizzi.

"Then give him a weapon," Zizzi said icily.

"Can't do that," Adam answered cheerily. "Besides, Commander Zizzi, how long has it been since you engaged in hand-to-hand combat? Give me the dagger."

"I was fighting Kamarians before you were born," Zizzi snapped. *"Give him a weapon."*

Adam sighed—a bit theatrically, I thought. "We have no daggers aboard this ship, Commander. What shall I give him? A zancthon-powered sustaining-action heat ray?"

I saw Justin gape at Adam. You could hear him thinking: *What the hell is a zancthon-powered sustaining-action heat ray?*

"Sounds fine to me," Fluth said grimly.

Zizzi suddenly whirled and stood with his back against the wardroom wall, facing the rest of us. The odds were seven to one against, but he wasn't going to hand over his dagger politely just because we asked him to, no siree.

This comic-opera scene had gone on long enough. "Oh,

for heaven's sake, Zizzi!" I burst out. "Do you think we brought you two men up here so you could *fight*? Do you think we'll *let* you fight? Why don't you *talk* to each other, for crying out loud!"

"Give Adam the dagger," Alison pleaded.

"Give me a weapon!" Fluth thundered.

"Give me room!" shouted Zizzi.

Fluth lunged toward Zizzi, but Ben intercepted him and wrestled him back. Adam helped hold the Kamarian commander, making terrible faces at being called upon to play the role of muscle man.

"Commander Zizzi!" cried Sondra. "Put, down, that, dagger!"

"Stand back!" Zizzi hissed.

Then Justin Bark did something we should have thought of at the beginning. He marched up to the Lodonite commander and assumed a military stance. "Commander Zizzi," he said briskly, "I call upon you to surrender your weapon. Your position is untenable. You are outnumbered and we possess the superior weaponry should we choose to use it. We offer you the chance to negotiate. The alternative is to deprive the Lodonite army of its commanding officer. Your weapon, please."

Zizzi surrendered the dagger.

"Disease," Ben Whitfield said patiently for the fourth or fifth time. "The time of weakness is caused by a disease. And it can be cured."

Zizzi and Fluth sat glowering at each across a wardroom table.

"There's no need for any Lodonite or Kamarian ever to suffer the time of weakness again," Ben went on. "If you'll both agree to cooperate and organize a program for getting your people treated, the Federation can come in and stop the disease."

Zizzi raised an eyebrow. "A disease that takes turns? First Lodon, then Kamaria, then Lodon again, then—"

"The disease travels with the bibblings. The birds carry both the cause and the cure. Commander Zizzi, you know this is Kamaria's time of weakness. Look at Commander

Fluth. He's as healthy as you are. He's living proof that the time of weakness can be stopped—we stopped it for *him*. We have a serum that does the job."

Zizzi examined his enemy carefully. "Is this true, Fluth?"

Fluth looked at Ben accusingly. "You didn't tell me you were going to cure the Lodonites too."

Sondra: "Too bad we had to threaten Zizzi before he'd give up his dagger. Do you think he really believed it? The threat, I mean. Do you think he really believed we'd—how did Justin put it? 'Deprive the Lodonite army of its commanding officer'? *I* think Zizzi was just looking for a graceful way out."

I agreed. "All that shouting and fumbling that was going on—no military man worth his salt could give in to that. Especially when his archenemy was a part of it."

"Well, whether he believed it or just pretended to believe it, it worked. At least they're talking to each other now."

"Liar!" shouted Fluth. "Lying, treacherous, murderous scum! It was the Lodonites who broke the first truce, not the Kamarians! Liar!"

Zizzi coolly appraised his ranting antagonist. "How would you know, Fluth? Kamarians can't remember back a full generation, much less eight. Do you keep records? Do you have even an oral tradition to keep the past alive? You believe what you want to believe. Kamarians have no regard for truth."

"Perhaps," said Adam, "this is one of those truths that are best kept buried in some remote and inaccessible spot. Whichever side was in the right, that means the other side was in the wrong. A new truce can't be built on that kind of inequality. Forget the first truce. Concentrate on this one."

"Forget!" Fluth was dumbfounded at the enormity of the suggestion. "Forget what the Lodonites have been doing to us all these years?"

Zizzi shook his head. "There are some things that just can't be forgotten, mirhilancthon Chester. Not ever."

"Well, there now," Adam said cheerfully. "You've agreed upon something! You both prefer to nurse a hatred that grew out of a disease that can now be cured. Makes perfect sense to me," he finished innocently.

Both commanders glared at him murderously.

"I have learned," Justin said judiciously, "that Adam Chester always knows what he's doing. I have also learned, I do not always understand what Adam Chester is always doing. Why is he mocking them? In my innocence I always thought belittling people was not the way to put them in a receptive frame of mind."

"That's mostly for Zizzi's sake," I said. "He has a better sense of the absurd than Fluth has. Adam's trying to provoke Zizzi, to make him acknowledge the absurdity of continuing the war when it's no longer necessary. Zizzi has to be the first to express a willingness to negotiate."

"Why's that?"

"Because Fluth is more likely to accept a situation than he is to create one. Zizzi'll be the first to come round. You'll see."

"I see Fluth is healthy," said Zizzi, "and so I cannot doubt that you have found a cure for the disease. But how can you blame the bibblings? When they are with us we are strong. It's only when they leave that we become . . . diseased."

Fluth listened to this and decided to look puzzled.

Alison: "The bibblings carry a—well, you have no word for it in your language. We call it a 'microorganism.' It's so small you can't see it with the naked eye. The bibblings leave it behind when they migrate and it makes you sick."

" 'The naked eye'?" said Fluth. "What is a 'naked' eye? And if this thing is too small to see, how do you know it's there?"

Alison smiled. "I can show it to you. Let's go to the lab."

Adam: "Let's go to the cabin, Val."

"Why?"

"Your pheromones are calling me."

"It's habit," said Sondra. "You have become *habituated* to your enmity. It's all you've ever known, and it's difficult to accept a complete about-face. It won't be easy, but it can be done. We want you to sign what's called an Agreement of Intent. All that means is that you're willing to cease hostilities long enough to make a try at negotiating a permanent peace."

Zizzi smiled. "You make it sound so simple, mirhiliptha. All we have to do is cease hostilities for a while, you say. But look at who that 'we' is. Lodon is in its time of strength right now—*we* are the ones who would be taking the risk. What you suggest would cost the Kamarians nothing. It could cost us the war."

"There needn't *be* any war if you'd just sign the agreement!"

"I do not believe in magic, mirhiliptha."

Sondra didn't even try to hide her exasperation. "If you'd sign right now, there might be time to get a disease-control operation in here before the end of your time of strength. So you wouldn't be risking anything—you'd retain your strength even after the bibblings leave Lodon. You and the Kamarians would be on an equal footing. Here's the Agreement of Intent—now stop dragging your feet and *sign* the bloody thing!"

" 'Bloody'?" said Zizzi.

Ben, grinning: "Alison wants to know if you'd like us to slip something into their food and drink to make them mellower and more amenable to suggestion."

"That's an idea," I laughed. "If we could be sure they wouldn't change their minds later."

"It's been six days now—any sign of progress?"

"Well, Zizzi is at least willing to talk, to try to explain his position. Fluth is playing a waiting game."

"So if Zizzi agrees to negotiate . . ."

"Fluth will follow his lead, I'm sure of it. Only he'll see it as 'resisting' to the last moment."

"Let him. Whatever it takes."

"You're fighting a war because you both want to follow the bibblings when they migrate," Justin said. "You want to follow the bibblings because you want to escape the time of weakness. Now that there's another way to stop the time of weakness, the need to fight over the bibblings disappears. Right so far?"

"Yes," said Zizzi. Fluth grunted noncommittally.

"Yet you both want to go on killing each other? Why? Do you enjoy it?"

Zizzi looked pained. "You do not need to point out the ridiculousness of the situation, mirhilancthon Bark. I am well aware of it. But you are wrong when you say we want to go on killing each other. Lodon wishes no such thing—but we have no choice when the only way out is to trust Kamarians to keep their word. Kamarians simply are not capable of keeping their word."

"Zizzi," roared Fluth, "I challenge you to combat!"

"Forget it," Justin said flatly. "You're both in neutral territory and there'll be no fighting on board this ship." He looked closely at the two commanders. "So it's solely the old matter of mutual distrust that's holding us up? Is that it? Neither one of you trusts the other to stop fighting even though the *reason* for fighting no longer exists? Well, how about this? What if the Federation sends in a watch-dog police force—a guard to patrol the mountains to make sure neither side breaks the agreement? Would that satisfy you?"

"Possibly," Zizzi mused. "I'd want to know specific details before I could agree."

Fluth grunted noncommittally.

"Time for the *coup de main*, I think," Adam said. "Are you ready?"

"Ready," I said.

Zizzi and Fluth were talking to each other when we

joined them in the wardroom—actually *talking*. Adam sat down next to Fluth and I slid into the seat next to Zizzi.

"We've thrown a lot of things at you during the past seven or eight days," I said to the two commanders, "and we thought we'd better try to put things into some kind of order. We'd like to tell you what *we* want to see happen. Then maybe you'd tell us what parts, if any, you object to. Adam?"

"We want you to stop fighting," he said simply. "Since agreeing to a truce is the real bone of contention, we'll just have to make an assumption for now. Assume you both sign the Agreement of Intent—what will happen next is this. First, the Federation will send in medical teams to cure the Kamarian men and women of the bibbling disease. Commander Fluth, you'll need to organize the neuters to help round up all the disease's victims. Second, the medical teams will treat the Lodonite men and women to prevent their catching the disease in the future—yes, Commander, it's possible," he said, noticing Zizzi's look of surprise. "It's called inoculation."

"How do you know it works, this . . . inoculation?" Fluth the skeptic.

"Commander," I said, "we came into Kamaria looking for you. During your time of weakness. How could we do that if we were not protected against the disease? We were inoculated before we left the ship."

Fluth swiveled his head toward Adam. "Is that right?" Fluth trusted Adam but he didn't quite trust me. Grr.

Adam: "Quite right."

"Perhaps you are naturally immune to our sickness?" Zizzi wondered.

"No, Commander," I said. "We are not immune." I told him five of us had caught the disease and that Justin Bark had saved us by following the bibblings.

Both Zizzi and Fluth looked stricken. "I'm sorry," Fluth blurted out. "I didn't know—I'm sorry." It was *their* disease and they had given it to us and Fluth felt responsible. Good man.

Zizzi was subdued. "You come here to help us and we respond by making you sick. We did not ask for your help, but you came anyway. And you persisted even through your own time of weakness." He looked over at the Kamarian Commander. "Fluth, we owe them the courtesy of listening."

Fluth made a sound that Adam interpreted as "yes." "After the medical teams have finished, we'll send in a guard to patrol the mountains and make sure both Lodon and Kamaria are keeping the agreement."

"Armed?" asked Fluth.

"Absolutely not," said Adam. "We don't expect you to allow armed aliens to walk in and take over. They'll be observers, that's all. They'll report any violations to the other side but they won't take action themselves."

Zizzi looked at me. "True?" So Zizzi trusted me but he didn't quite trust Adam. Grr again.

"Quite true."

"The guard will be withdrawn anytime you say," Adam went on, "or we can skip it entirely if you decide it's not necessary. It's available if you want it, while you're negotiating the terms of a permanent peace. And for the negotiations themselves, the Federation is willing to provide any help you want. All you have to do is ask. Anything at all."

Zizzi cleared his throat. "At the risk of sounding ungrateful, this is the part that puzzles me. Why is the Federation willing to do all this? Your presence here now must be at tremendous expense—and the Federation is willing to go even farther, to provide medical teams, mountain observers, help with the negotiations. Why?"

"They want us to join the Federation," Fluth said.

"Exactly right," I said. "We want you to join the Federation."

"I assumed that was your ultimate goal," Zizzi the sharpie said, "but I still must ask why? Why is the Federation so interested in us?"

Here it was.

"Money," I said bluntly. "You don't know it, but that world you live on is a rich, rich planet. Lodon-Kamaria has extensive deposits of a mineral called alphidium, which is a source of energy the Federation depends upon heavily. It can provide heat, light, power—this very ship you're in is powered by an alphidium derivative. And there are tons of the stuff down there just waiting to be mined. We're here to make a deal. It's that simple."

Zizzi's eyes were gleaming. "Yes . . . yes, it makes sense now. A deal. Business. Of course."

"But we can't do business so long as Lodonites and Kamarians are in the business of killing each other. I'll give you one guess as to where the alphidium is located."

Zizzi and Fluth exchanged a look. Together: "The mountains."

"Right. The Federation is willing to finance a mining operation with a percentage of the profits going to Lodon and Kamaria. We'll get the alphidium, you'll get rich, and everybody will be happy. But none of these good things are going to happen if you go on with the war. You no longer have a reason to fight—the disease can be stopped. And now you have a reason *not* to fight. So, how about it?"

Fluth poked Adam. "Did she say 'rich'?"

"She said 'rich,'" Adam laughed. "Like the sound of that?"

"I like it," Fluth said, and actually smiled.

"Why didn't you tell us about the alphidium before now?" Zizzi wanted to know.

"You wouldn't have believed us," I said. "You'd have thought it was some kind of trick. Have you noticed how often you're saying 'we' and 'us' now? That had to come first."

"So the Federation's motives—"

"Are purely commercial. You've got something they want, they're willing to pay for it. A deal."

"That I can trust," smiled Fluth, and nodded at me.

"You're a manipulator, mirhiliptha Valerie Chester," Zizzi said wryly.

"I know," I admitted, "and it bothers me when I let myself think about it. Would you rather we'd just turned around and gone back home?"

"No, certainly not," he smiled. "You have saved us

from the time of weakness. That overrides everything. We will be forever grateful to you."

"Not too grateful," Adam said hastily. "Remember the neuters. By the way, don't take the first offer the Federation makes you. Don't even take their *tenth* offer. Hold out as long as you can—make 'em pay through the nose."

Zizzi looked vaguely puzzled that Adam should be offering this advice, but nodded agreement.

"Before you label us total villains," I said to Zizzi, "let me point out there was another way we could have ended the war, a much faster way. A way we chose not to follow."

He understood. "By force. Federation arms and troops. I thought of that the first time I saw you, standing outside your shuttle, waiting to meet us. It was the *very* first thing that came to my mind."

I laid my hand on his arm. "Now put it out of your mind. Don't think of it ever again. We would never have decided to use force, mining rights or no mining rights. In our own clumsy manipulative way, we were simply trying to help. That's all we ever wanted to do. Help."

Zizzi put his hand over mine. "I know that, Valerie. I've always known that. You don't have to tell me."

"If you're going to make love to my wife," Adam said, "you could at least wait until I'm out of the room. What do you think, Fluth? Shouldn't he wait until I'm out of the room?"

"I think he should wait until you're *both* out of the room," said Fluth.

A joke! Commander Fluth made a joke!

"Well, Fluth?" said Zizzi.

"Well, Zizzi?" said Fluth.

Two days later they signed the Agreement of Intent.

Epilogue

Culloden closed his eyes upward and folded his hands in his lap. "Yes, it really is too bad about the bibblings. It must have been a great shock to the Lodonites and the Kamarians—since it was more than just a sentimental attachment on their part. I think they took it very well, considering."

Considering their world had been turned upside down. "I'm not sure they all understood, Director," I said. "Or even believed us. All they had was our say-so."

He raised a long thin finger. "Supported by the word of Zizzi and Fluth. *And* the fact that we did succeed in stopping the disease. But as you say, there'll always be some who don't understand. But time will be our ally. In time, they will all accept it."

That wasn't quite what I'd said, but I didn't belabor the point. Culloden knew the difference.

"I think they already accept it," Adam said carefully, "even if they don't quite understand it. These are very pragmatic people, Director—especially the Kamarians. Lodonites are more inclined to ask questions, if I may be permitted so sweeping a generalization."

"And we shall answer their questions," Culloden said complacently. "Perhaps an information-dispersal center? They must have questions about more than just the bibblings. Two centers—one on each side of the mountains. Yes, something like that is needed. Remind me to look into it when we get back, Pilcer."

158

"Yes, Director," said his assistant. "An excellent idea."

It was almost two years to the day since we'd returned to Corps Headquarters waving the signed Agreement of Intent in our hot little hands. Peace negotiations had proceeded rapidly, and a stunned Lodonite-Kamarian populace had learned three things in quick succession. First, the time of weakness was gone forever. Second, the war was over. Third, they all had a chance to get rich quick. Heady stuff for a world ranked only 5.1 on the Denner scale of social development.

Once the necessary treaties were signed, the Federation moved in, first with medical teams to manufacture large quantities of the anti-X serum and inject it into the disease's victims. By then the bibblings had migrated again, and it took the teams about two months to track down all the infected Lodonites. Then the Kamarians were inoculated, and the Federation was at last satisfied everyone on the planet had been treated.

The returning medical teams had unanimously recommended that the bibblings be exterminated.

The Whitfields and the Barks and Adam and I were on a planet in the Albireo system when we heard the news. We'd had three easy missions after Lodon-Kamaria, one of them lasting only two weeks. We were shocked when we learned that the Federation had decided that interfering with the bibblings' migratory pattern by redistributing the food supply was too time-consuming and too troublesome a procedure. Just kill 'em off, that'll show the little buggers!

But the Whitfields, not really surprisingly, had agreed with the decision to wipe out the species. "Disease is tricky," Alison had said. "Sometimes it'll allow itself to be controlled so well that we think it's been eliminated, when in fact it's only gone into hiding for a while. A case in point is the epidemic of bubonic plague on Earth in 1995 and '96. Earth should have learned from past experience. The plague had already lain dormant once before for a period of eight hundred years before it re-emerged as virulent as ever. Earth should have been prepared for that. The same thing could happen with the bibbling disease, don't you see? Anti-X might work only until the X organism develops a resistance."

"Which is not only possible but probable," Ben had added. "The disease has been around for eight generations now. A resistant strain could develop at any time. The surest way of controlling it is to get rid of the carrier."

So the decontamination ships were the next to arrive at Lodon-Kamaria, laying down an oily cloud of something called Thanos-17, guaranteed to rid the planet of its disease-carrying bibblings. The golden birds began falling out of the air in midflight, falling out of trees, falling off friendly shoulders. Thanos-17 did its job: in two days all the bibblings were dead.

Thanos-17 did something else as well: it permanently damaged the Lodonite-Kamarian Z chromosome. In less than a year no more neuters were being born. Garrinel, Glawklug: the last of their kind. A lifetime from now the Lodonite and Kamarian populations would consist of men and women only, just like us.

Before the newly allied Lodonites and Kamarians had finished clearing the dead bibblings from their land, the first of the mining ships had arrived. Federation power-supply stations were erected at carefully selected spots on the planet; the Lodonites and Kamarians were allowed to tap in for only slightly extortionate fees. Life no longer ground to a halt when darkness fell, and with that simple change a centuries-old pattern of living yielded to a new kind of life. The "natives" were jerked forward a thousand years into a technological future without the benefit of any kind of period of transition. A new rivalry sprang up between Lodon and Kamaria, this one based on profit. Just like us.

"I had so hoped the Kamarians and Lodonites would be able to come to some sort of political agreement," the Culloden remarked. "A united land after so much dissension—it would have been a fitting conclusion."

"They could have called themselves Lodarians," Pilcer said, only half-facetiously. "Maybe they'll see the advantages of uniting yet."

"One government is so much easier to negotiate with than two," his superior murmured. "Especially when the two don't really trust each other."

"Perhaps they didn't understand how much they were inconveniencing us," Justin Bark said expressionlessly.

Culloden shot him a glance and decided not to pick up on it. "Of course there's one undeniable advantage in having them maintain their individual states. They're bound to vie with each other over the years as to which can offer the Federation the best prices, the best services, and so on. It might be better for us in the long run if things remain the way they are. We'll see."

Yes, we certainly would see, all right. We were on our way to Lodon-Kamaria now for the formal ceremonies that would admit the small planet to membership in the Federation of United Worlds. This was no small-time JX-31 we were traveling in, but a luxury ship carrying members of the Federation Council as well as other dignitaries from the Diplomatic Corps. The fact that Culloden was making the journey himself instead of just sending Pilcer showed how important the occasion was. And no wonder: a second deposit of alphidium had been found in one of the uninhabited continents of Lodon-Kamaria.

"Divide and conquer," said Justin. "A price war can be just as good as the other kind."

I think Culloden would have raised an eyebrow if he'd had one. I looked at that smooth white face, that shimmering white robe, the white hands folded in his lap. So composed, so sure of what he was and where he was going. How much did he understand of what had happened to Justin? How much did he want to understand?

For a time there I thought we were going to lose Justin. The disgust he'd felt at the fate of the neuters made him seriously consider resigning from the Corps. No one wanted him to quit. Resourceful, energetic, rightheaded—Justin was the very kind of person we needed. He also happened to be *a nice guy*. A foolish reason for wanting him to stay? No. A very important reason. Adam talked to him for hours on end—reasoning, cajoling, persuading.

It was touch-and-go there for a while, but he bounced back—and he bounced back with a vengeance. Justin's face is harder now, and he makes decisions more quickly than he used to. He's acquired the kind of "tolerance" that comes to one who has decided the only realistic goal is to make the best of an inevitably bad situation. *Expect the worst.* He has a brilliant career ahead of him.

Culloden: "I don't think we need worry about the Lodonites and the Kamarians, do you? They'll not only survive, they'll prosper. They're a strong people—and we'll be stronger because of them. Look how well they took the news that their neuter line would die out in another generation. I don't mind telling you, I was expecting quite an uproar over that! But no, they accepted it just as philosophically as they accepted all the other changes that have come about on their world. Rather surprising, in a way."

Not so surprising. What we should have expected, in fact. I could imagine the enormous sigh of relief that must have gone up over the entire planet. The Lodonites and the Kamarians were at last free of their terrible burden of gratitude.

Adam activated a viewport. We sat silently for a while, watching Lodon-Kamaria grow from pinhead to melon size. It was the same world we'd left two years ago, and it wasn't the same world we'd left two years ago.

Culloden stirred. "We'll be in orbit soon. Are you in the first shuttle, Valerie?"

"The second."

"You'll have a little more time then. I'm in the first— so if you'll excuse me, I'd like to change. I've been advised that modest apparel is preferred on Lodon-Kamaria. Is that correct?"

"On the whole. Zizzi has an eye for elegance, though."

"Oh, has he? I'll keep that in mind. It's better not to wear the same thing for meeting both ex-commanders anyway, don't you think?" He gave his eye-slit smile and left.

"Men," sighed Sondra. "Always thinking about clothes."

Fluth's new headquarters building was everything that Federation plastic could make it. The former army commander sat behind a semicircular desk covered with reports on the activities of Kamarian Mining Enterprises, of which he was the head. He looked happy.

We'd waited until Culloden and the other VIPs had made their official visit, and now Fluth greeted Adam like a long-lost brother. He even seemed glad to see the rest of us. When the preliminary greetings were over, he said what was on his mind in his usual blunt fashion. He offered Adam a job.

"I need a liaison man," Fluth said. "Someone not appointed by the Federation but who knows the ins and outs of Federation policy. They've sent me some assistants—good men, good men, every one of them. But they're working for the Federation, not me. I want an eye and an ear where they'll count most—inside the inner circle of power, you understand? What do you think?"

Adam managed to work up a semblance of enthusiasm as he thanked Fluth for the offer, and declined. "You need someone more directly connected with the Federation Council, Fluth. All my ties are with the Diplomatic Corps. And they're strong ties, I might add. I don't want to break them."

Fluth shot me a glance and said hurriedly, "No need to break them. Plenty of jobs here, lots of work to be done. I can use all six of you—you'll still be a team, heh? But now a team working for Kamaria. How does that sound to you?"

It sounded to me as if Fluth had turned into a blustery corporation man. I was beginning to feel ill.

Fluth made Adam promise to think about his offer, and then changed the subject. He talked at length about the changes taking place in Kamaria, how the face of the land was changing because of the new wealth that had already started to flow in. Changes that Fluth insisted on crediting to *us*. He really wanted Adam.

"There's one change we regret," Alison said tightly. "We had no idea our actions would result in the neuter line's dying out. I can't tell you how deeply sorry we are."

Fluth immediately assumed a somber mien. "Yes, most unfortunate, most unfortunate. But then, you could say they've outlived their function now. We no longer have any need for neuters in Kamaria."

Justin turned away.

"It must be painful for you," I said, perversely ignoring a warning signal from Adam. "Seeing them die out when you know how much you owe them. For keeping the race alive. During the time of weakness."

"What? Oh yes—but that's all in the past now, all in the past."

How quickly.

"Fluth, what are all these interesting-looking circles and squares and triangles you've got scattered hither and yon?" Adam, staring purposefully at a mounted diagram of the Kamarian mining operation. Determined to save the visit.

Fluth took his time joining Adam at the diagram; you could see him choosing his words carefully. "The circles, the squares, and the triangles," he said slowly, "each indicate a different kind of digging operation. The circles mark our tunnels that cross the line that divides our side of the mountains from Lodon's. We feel that whoever originates the tunnel has the right to work it to the end of the vein. The matter's in arbitration now."

A corner of Sondra's mouth twitched. "Have you stopped work in the tunnels?"

Fluth, affably: "Oh, we couldn't do that. Lose too much time. The Federation arbitrators will decide in our favor, I'm sure of it."

"Even though you're tunneling into Lodonite territory?"

Fluth's voice took on a defensive edge. "Why should we uncover a vein and then turn it over to the Lodonites? Business is business, mirhiliptha. It's the movers who make the profit."

Adam murmured something about a cooperative effort and asked about the squares on the diagram.

Fluth's defensiveness evaporated in an instant, and he

chuckled. "Those are diversionary tunnels." He chuckled again.

Ben peered over Adam's shoulder. "What are diversionary tunnels?"

"Tunnels on the other side of the dividing line. They contain just enough alphidium to make the Lodonites think a rich vein lies nearby."

"Alphidium that you've placed there?" Ben couldn't quite keep his voice neutral. "You're salting the mine?"

Fluth's defensiveness returned. "Where do you think we learned such a trick? From the Lodonites, that's where! They misled us two, three times. We have to defend ourselves!"

They started it, they did it first, it's their fault. The same old refrain—echoed on the other side of the mountains as well? Lodon-Kamaria hadn't changed as much as Fluth liked to think it had.

"I can't wait to hear what the triangles are," Justin, sardonically. *Expect the worst.*

Fluth wouldn't tell us what the triangles were.

I was glad when the visit ended. The temperature had cooled considerably, but Fluth repeated his offer to Adam. The former commander and his fellow Kamarians had been setting traps for the Lodonites for so long that they just couldn't stop now. They'd simply switched from one kind of conflict to another. They'd traded one kind of sickness for another. All that was missing were the bibblings.

Zizzi had announced his retirement.

"Time to step aside and let younger people take over," he smiled. "I think I've earned a rest."

He was living in a sprawling stone house in an area isolated from the mining operation, not far from Lodon's eastern shoreline. The place had probably housed Lodonite children during the time of weakness.

"I can't believe you've retired," I said. "You're too full of ginger for that."

When I explained what "full of ginger" meant, he laughed. "Well, I do have an advisory position on the governing board of the mining operation," he said, "but nobody's asked my advice yet."

So they didn't want him. Their brightest and their best, and they'd put him out to pasture.

What I was thinking must have showed on my face, because Zizzi hastened to add, "I want it this way, Valerie. It gives me time to do something I've thought about doing for a long time. Look here. I'm writing a history of Lodon-Kamaria."

Justin the ex-historian: front and center, full of questions. Zizzi showed him what he was doing, and stopped to marvel over a machine the rest of us had been using all our lives.

"A most remarkable machine," Zizzi said. "A gift from the Federation Council. All I have to do is flip this switch"—he did—"depress this button, and look what happens." The voicewriter's screen read *Depress this button and look what happens.* "At first I thought I'd write my memoirs," Zizzi went on, flipping off the machine, "but then I decided I ought to try to assemble some sort of overall record of what went on here before the Chester Commission arrived. That is correct, isn't it? The Chester Commission? It's the term your Director Culloden uses."

Justin offered to translate the history into English.

Zizzi accepted. "It isn't only our country that's changing," he remarked. "Our language is changing too, absorbing words from your language that we've never needed before. Technical terms, of course, but other words and phrases as well. Wage control. Demographics. Industrial espionage." He paused. "Sabotage."

We were silent a moment and then Alison said, "May we ask who's responsible for the sabotage?"

Zizzi spread his hands. "If the word is uttered angrily, then it's the Kamarians who are responsible. If it's spoken furtively, then my fellow Lodonites must be the guilty ones. I don't know how extensive the sabotage is, or how efficacious. But it has begun."

Adam: "Is anything being done to stop it?"

"Not that I know of. Some sort of policing action may

be in the works—I'm afraid I've lost touch with things since I moved out here."

"*You* could run such an operation," I said.

"Perhaps once I could have. Now, I'm not so sure—the changes in Lodon are so drastic. But the question doesn't really arise. That sort of decision is out of my hands now."

"Have you offered your services?"

"No."

How unemotional his utterance of that word was: containing neither hesitancy nor defiance. Simply *no,* a statement of a conclusion reached. Zizzi's youthful dream of a peaceful and disease-free existence for his country had come true, long after he himself had concluded it was only a foolish daydream. But the pleasures, the *rewards*—where were they? This should be a time of exultation for Zizzi, a time of triumph! Instead he'd retreated from the new life he'd helped create, to this lonely spot far from the center of Lodon's hustle and bustle. Like the neuters, Zizzi too had outlived his function. The brave new world had no place for him.

I was glad when this visit too came to an end.

"He's given up," I said to Adam when we'd left. "He's just given up."

Adam slipped his arm around my shoulders and gave me an encouraging hug but said nothing. There was nothing to be said.

Ritual time had arrived.

Bigdaddy Federation opening its thousand arms to welcome the newest member of the family. Solemnifying an occasion: how we love it! That's one thing that will never change. We love reaffirming our worth, our significance, our very existence. *We're alive and we've got this here ceremony to prove it.*

Gathered together: Zizzi, Fluth, officials of both mining operations, Council members, diplomats, minions, flunkies, gofers.

And Culloden. "How very proud you must be, Valerie. A world saved from itself and started on the road toward the future. Health and prosperity. And it was your team that made it possible. What terrible lives these people must have lived before you came—well, I don't have to tell you, do I? You experienced their time of weakness for yourself. That must have been dreadful for you."

"Yes, it was," I said, perhaps too emphatically. "But it was even worse for the Lodonites and the Kamarians. *It had to be stopped.*"

Culloden looked at me querulously. "But of course it had to be stopped. No one questions that. My dear Valerie, do I detect a note of regret?"

"No, not really. They couldn't go on living that way. But it just strikes me that what we've done here is a trifle . . . graceless."

He understood. "Ah yes, perfection in all things— wouldn't it be nice? But we both know that's impossible. What you're saying is that we should have come a little closer to it than we did. A great deal closer, if I understand you correctly. But we do the best we can. Don't underestimate your achievement here. Look around—what do you see? Healthy people working at bettering their lives. That's no small accomplishment. And they *will* better their lives—both countries are competitive, they're not afraid of sharp business practices, they show a remarkably acute grasp of the world of commerce they're entering. They have uncanny powers of adaptation."

"How fortunate for everybody."

Culloden answered my tone instead of my words. "Lodon and Kamaria are what they are. These two nations are destined to fight each other. Why shouldn't that fight be made profitable for everyone concerned?" Eye-slit smile. "Well, shall we go? The ceremonies are about to begin. Be proud, Valerie. Look around you and see what you have done. This is your day."

Our day. Something to remember, something to be proud of. Something to comfort us in our old age.

Chalk up one more for the Anglo-Saxon Invaders.

ABOUT THE AUTHOR

BARBARA PAUL has an M.A. in English, a
Ph.D. in theater history, and before becoming
a refugee from the groves of academe, she
taught at the University of Pittsburgh. Since
abandoning university life, Barbara has worked
as a technical writer, a book reviewer, and a
movie critic. She is the author of several science
fiction novels, including PILLARS OF SALT,
which is available in a Signet edition. Barbara
Paul lives in Pittsburgh.

SIGNET Science Fiction You'll Enjoy

☐ **BEYOND THE BEYOND** by Poul Anderson.
(#W7760—$1.50)
☐ **THE DANCER FROM ATLANTIS** by Poul Anderson.
(#W7806—$1.50)
☐ **THE DAY OF THEIR RETURN** by Poul Anderson.
(#W7941—$1.50)
☐ **THE PEOPLE OF THE WIND** by Poul Anderson.
(#W7900—$1.50)
☐ **THE BOOK OF SKULLS** by Robert Silverberg.
(#W7385—$1.50)
☐ **DOWNWARD TO THE EARTH** by Robert Silverberg.
(#W7134—$1.50)
☐ **NEW DIMENSIONS, IV** by Robert Silverberg.
(#Y6113—$1.25)
☐ **THOSE WHO WATCH** by Robert Silverberg.
(#W8149—$1.50)
☐ **A TIME OF CHANGES** by Robert Silverberg.
(#W7386—$1.50)
☐ **THE BLACK CLOUD** by Fred Hoyle.   (#W7833—$1.50)*
☐ **CASE AND THE DREAMER** by Theodore Sturgeon.
(#W7933—$1.50)
☐ **THE BEST OF TREK®** edited by Walter Irwin and G. B. Love.
(#E8030—$1.75)
☐ **THE DEMOLISHED MAN** by Alfred Bester.
(#Y7585—$1.25)
☐ **EYE AMONG THE BLIND** by Robert Holdstock.
(#E8480—$1.75)*
☐ **LORD TYGER** by Philip José Farmer.   (#W7577—$1.50)
* Not available in Canada

Buy them at your local bookstore or use this convenient coupon for ordering.

THE NEW AMERICAN LIBRARY, INC.,
P.O. Box 999, Bergenfield, New Jersey 07621

Please send me the SIGNET BOOKS I have checked above. I am enclosing
$_____ (please add 50¢ to this order to cover postage and handling).
Send check or money order—no cash or C.O.D.'s. Prices and numbers are
subject to change without notice.

Name _____

Address _____

City_____ State_____ Zip Code_____
Allow 4-6 weeks for delivery.
This offer is subject to withdrawal without notice.